DARK SACRED NIGHT

E.S. TAYLOR

EAST RIDGE PUBLISHING

DARK SACRED NIGHT

No animal could ever be so cruel as a man, so artfully, so artistically cruel.
— Fyodor Dostoyevsky, *The Brothers Karamazov*

1

S amuel felt the swell and release of Tess's body from his position behind her. A sign of resignation, he knew. A rare show of emotion.

The mare had picked up a hitch a couple of hours ago, a slight unevenness in her gait that had now developed into a limp.

Samuel had known this was coming. His own mount had gone down the day before—exhaustion or dehydration, or both—leaving Tess and him no choice but to share her horse. Samuel also knew the clock had started ticking then; there'd be no way to stay ahead of them anymore, no realistic chance at a feign or misdirection, and no chance at all to outrun them. And though she'd never show it, he was certain Tess realized it as well.

Tess dismounted and took a long look over her shoulder, toward the ground they'd already covered, before turning back to the horse and loosening the straps on her saddlebags.

She withdrew the paper, the same single page he'd seen

her studying and scribbling on countless times over the past week. Samuel had once risked a peek over her shoulder as she wrote, but he couldn't make out any of the words. Even though he'd worked hard on his letters several years ago, the script seemed alien to him.

Tess scanned the page quickly this time, making neither addition nor subtraction. Then she produced a rock and length of twine from her pack, carefully wrapped the paper around the rock and secured it with the twine.

"What are you doing?" Samuel asked.

Tess didn't answer. Instead, she pivoted and hurled the paper over the precipice behind them, a sheer drop of fifty or sixty feet to the forest and river below.

Samuel watched as she studied the trees and under-growth near the rim of the drop-off, the familiar fierce concentration in her eyes.

There were wisps of white in her dirty-blond hair now, leaking around the brim of her hat like wet straw in the sunlight. He hadn't noticed that before, but he liked it. It suited her, as did her accent—which was also foreign to him. He realized he'd never asked where she was from.

"What are you doing?" he asked again.

Her focus broke slowly from the area where the paper had disappeared. "We kept our promise," she said. "We did the best we could."

She'd never told him what the promise was.

"I didn't come because of that." Samuel motioned in the direction she'd tossed the paper. "I came because of you."

She pursed her lips—a grin; her grin. She said, "I wondered if you'd ever say that."

"I mean it."

Tess gestured at the forest. "Go now. You still have some time. Put as much distance as you can between them and you. You might tire them in those trees and brush. Maybe they'll quit if you make them work."

"They haven't quit yet."

"They're not after you."

Samuel waited, and when she offered nothing more, he said, "I don't want it this way. I want to choose how it ends."

Tess glanced down at her revolvers, seemed to think about it. She was the only person he'd ever known who carried two pistols and was efficient with both. She didn't possess the speed of some, but rather an uncanny grace—a thing as beautiful as it was terrible to behold, like an experienced dancer or artist, or butcher.

She said, "I've seen this, what's about to happen here, but I haven't seen anything else." She paused, her attention turning inward. Then: "No, this is a good ending."

Before Samuel could protest, she turned and faced the area from which they'd come, the gentle ridge concealing the large clearing beyond. She said, "I've had a long life. My mother was only twenty-six when she died."

"Come on, Tess. You're—what?—in your thirties?"

"I don't know. I'd guess somewhere in my forties now, old enough to feel myself slowing."

"You'll never slow."

She looked away like he'd struck at something, another leak of emotion.

But then her eyes narrowed and hardened again, and

Samuel turned as the faint pulse of hoofbeats began rising over the ridge.

They were closer than he'd thought. But there couldn't be too many. Zalen wouldn't have sent more than four or five from the group. Which was still plenty, but there was always a chance with Tess. He'd seen her handle near as many before.

"Are you afraid?" Samuel asked.

Tess nodded, a slight dip of her hat. "But I'm afraid of living too."

That's not what Samuel had meant, and definitely not what he'd wanted to hear.

He turned back to the ridge and watched as the group emerged in a single file line and started to fan out.

He began counting: *one, two, three, four …*

BRAN STARTED WHISPERING when they heard the voice above them. *"If I'm still, it'll pass by. If I'm still, it'll pass by."*

Piper clamped a hand over her younger brother's mouth, hoping she wouldn't get bit this time. "Ain't nothing gonna pass by with you making all that racket. Now *shush it*!"

He'd gotten the line from their grandpa in the last days of his sickness. Grandpa had whispered the phrase over and over as well, night after night, on and on. But for all the repetition, whatever "*it*" was hadn't passed Grandpa by. It had taken him with it.

Bran screamed into her hand when something heavy thumped into the ground behind them and began rolling

LUKE JOYNER APPEARED a minute and a half later, as usual riding one of his father's formidable studs. He was early today and Virginia had a hunch she knew why, which soured her stomach. She nevertheless appreciated the boy. She'd known his elderly father Ephraim her whole life. And now that her own father had passed, Ephraim had been sending his young son over to help with the workload. Virginia was glad to have him. And she wasn't.

Luke pulled up, dismounted, and led his horse through the gate.

"Afternoon, Ms. Cooper."

"Luke."

Virginia noted the way he was dressed—not formal, but not his usual coveralls either. This reinforced her hunch.

The boy worked his father's place in the mornings and then used whatever remained of the day to help Virginia. It had started a year ago—two, maybe three times a week. Recently it had become daily.

Luke withdrew a thick fold of butcher paper. "Father sent this for you, ma'am. It's jerked beef."

Virginia nodded toward the house. "Just set it on the table. And give him my thanks."

Luke looked down, nudged a rock with his foot.

"Something else?" Virginia asked.

"I was wondering if I might call on Piper?"

Virginia gestured over her shoulder. "She'd better be down in that barn doing her chores, lest she get the switch."

Neither Piper nor Bran had ever received the switch, but Virginia found the threat an effective deterrent.

Luke didn't move. "I mean, I was thinking maybe after supper Piper might take kindly to a walk along the river.

The moonlight and sound of the water can be soothing after a day of labor."

Virginia wondered how long it took him to come up with that one.

Piper was developing early, as had Virginia and her mother before her—at least that's what Virginia had been told. And a girl entering womanhood, at any age, drew men's attention and fancy no less than a corral of fine horses, and for similar reasons.

Virginia went back to work on the fence post. "You're welcome to stay and eat supper with us. Then you can leave your horse in the corral and walk back home by the river in the moonlight and any other such thing that tickles your fancy."

Luke's disappointment was obvious from the sound of his voice, even as he did his best to disguise it. "Why, yes, ma'am, I'd love to take supper with your family tonight. Thank you for the invitation."

Virginia grinned, though her back was to him now. Luke was only a year older than Piper, and despite such things being largely out of her control, inevitable even, she didn't have to make it easy.

She expelled the thought, however, not just because she didn't want to think about it—which she didn't—but because the echoes of hooves had returned.

And this time it was not a single rider.

Virginia stood. Cotton had also turned his attention to the western edge of the property, toward the sound of approaching horses.

Virginia said, "Cotton."

"Yes'um?"

"Go down to the barn and keep the children there with you."

Cotton dropped his hammer and pliers and moved away.

To Luke, she said, "Go on now."

"Ms. Cooper—"

"*Get!*"

This time Virginia did go to her horse.

BRAN SAID, "Back there you said '*they're*' going to hear us, but I only heard one person. How'd you know there was more than one?"

"'Cause if someone's talking," Piper said, "that means someone's listening too. People don't just talk to themselves."

"Grandpa did."

Piper didn't know what to say to that. "Just get back to work before Mama finds out we've been roaming."

She peered through the crack in the barn door, felt the heft of the thing in her pocket bump against the wood frame. She wished her grandpa was still here, even in his later state. Grandpa was the smartest person she'd ever known. And though she hadn't yet looked at the strange object in her pocket, didn't know if she even should, she knew Grandpa would have the answer. He always knew what to do in a pinch.

She *definitely* couldn't tell her mom.

Bran said, "You gotta work too."

Upon arriving home, Piper hadn't seen anyone outside except her mom and Cotton—her mom's ranch hand. And now even he was gone, which wasn't surprising. He was known to take flight at the sound of a strong wind. No matter. Cotton was dumb as an ear of corn anyway. He wouldn't be any help.

She wondered if Cotton or her mom had heard the earlier rolls of thunder, because they hadn't sounded like thunder to her. She knew Bran, in his panicked condition, hadn't heard anything; otherwise, he'd be going on and on about it.

She patted her pocket and thought of retreating to an empty stall to examine the thing she'd found. But then she saw Cotton walking toward the barn.

Bran said, "You've gotta work too."

Piper waved a hand at her brother. Cotton was still coming but seemed distracted by something now, which also wasn't surprising. The man was thick as a bull moose and as smart as one too. Even *Bran* could do his sums. Cotton couldn't count to three if he was using his fingers. When he wasn't turning bits of wood into animals with his carving knife, the big man was known to stare at the woods for hours on end. Truth was, he made Piper nervous.

She said, "Cotton's coming."

"Good. Maybe he'll help us."

"He might tell on us too."

"He won't," Bran said. Then: "I don't think he can."

"Just keep working."

"You've gotta—"

"I know."

Before moving away Piper took a final peek through the crack in the door. Cotton wasn't out there anymore, or at least she couldn't see him.

That's when the voice rose behind her from the rear entrance of the barn.

"*You kids come on out of there.*"

It wasn't Cotton.

THREE RIDERS, all men, all looking haggard. None of whom Virginia recognized.

She slung the strap of the shotgun over her shoulder and met them at the gate. "Gentlemen, this is the Cooper ranch. I'm Virginia—"

"We don't give three shits who you are, lady," one of the men said. "And we damn sure ain't given to pleasantries."

The three men had fallen into a formation of two in the front and one in the rear. The two in the front had roaming eyes and were both bearded—one blond; one dark, flecked with gray. It was the blond who'd spoken.

The guy in the rear, who was neither bearded nor appraising her like the other two, eyed her shotgun. He gestured at something behind her. "Just so you know where you stand, ma'am."

Virginia turned and saw a man leading Cotton up from the direction of the barn, and yet another man guiding Piper and Bran. Cotton's wrists were bound in front of him with bailing twine.

Virginia said, "What is this?"

The guy in the rear didn't answer.

To Cotton, the blond said, "Hey, boy, fetch me some water from that well yonder."

Cotton stopped and the guy trailing behind shoved him with his rifle.

Cotton didn't move, didn't lift his head.

"What'd he say?" the blond asked.

The man behind Cotton laughed. "Can't understand him for shit, but he sure sounds angry."

The blond reached for his rifle.

Virginia threw up a hand. "Don't you dare."

The blond narrowed his eyes. "What'd you say to me, woman?"

"He's simple," Virginia said quickly. "He don't know what you're asking."

The blond glanced at Cotton.

"Just state your intentions," Virginia said.

Piper and Bran hurried over to her side, but Virginia pushed them away. "Go wait in the house."

"Whoa, now," the dark-haired man said. "Turn around there for me, little lady."

Piper glanced behind her. "What do you mean, mister?"

"I mean, give me a little whirl."

Piper looked at Virginia.

"I said turn around, girl!" the dark-haired man shouted.

Piper flinched, then did a quick twirl. "Like that?"

The blond whistled. "Hell, if you was just a bit further along …"

The dark-haired man angled his horse toward Piper. "I'd say she's ripe enough."

Virginia raised her shotgun. "No closer." Then to the children: "I said get to the house."

"Nobody moves," the guy in the rear said.

Virginia saw all three men had also raised their weapons, and she had no doubt the two behind her had as well.

She also noticed the blackness behind the dark-haired

man's eyes. She knew that void in a man, that vacancy of a soul.

The man said, "Nobody points a gun at me, lady."

The man in the rear said, "*Cyrus* ..."

"But I'm gonna give you a chance to apologize," Cyrus said. "Me and you are going to mosey down to that barn back there and—"

"Cyrus!"

Cyrus turned. "There something you want to say to me, Hux?"

Hux said, "Unless you'd rather I said it to Zalen."

Virginia slid back a step. She looked toward the western edge of the property, then searched the horizon behind the men at the gate.

Cyrus faced Virginia again. To Hux, he said, "Zee ain't against creature comforts."

"Zalen assigned us a job," Hux said. "Comforts come later."

Cyrus waved a hand dismissively, said, "Hell with you, Hux." But he didn't come any closer.

Hux said, "Ma'am, you said this is the Cooper place?"

"Just state your intentions," Virginia said again.

"And you are Ms. Cooper?"

"I'm Virginia Cooper."

"Ms. Cooper, please lower that scattergun. A weapon like that keeps everyone around it on edge."

Virginia did, slowly. She could feel her heart beating in her throat now; she also sensed the other two men easing in behind her.

Hux said, "Now toss it over the fence here."

She couldn't do that, couldn't will her hands to release the weapon.

Hux angled his head toward the children. "Consider your actions carefully, Ms. Cooper."

Virginia saw the man behind her place a hand on Bran's shoulder.

She lowered the hammers on the shotgun and tossed it over the fence.

"Much obliged," Hux said. "We're here because of the strangers who stopped by earlier. We need to collect what they left."

"Ain't nobody been by here today."

"Ma'am, honesty will serve you better than anything else right now. You see, we know some of our friends came through here earlier, and we know they left something behind."

"Ain't nobody been here."

"We saw the tracks, Ms. Cooper."

Virginia thought of Luke. "Those belong to the help."

Hux glanced at Cotton.

"That's the truth," Virginia said.

Hux thought about it. "I'm sure it is. But you'll understand, we'll need to have a look for ourselves."

"And then?"

Cyrus said, "And then you—"

"And then we leave," Hux said.

Cyrus set his jaw, but he also grinned at Virginia and winked at Piper.

Virginia looked over her shoulder. She noticed Cotton had backed away a few steps, no doubt ready to take flight like he was prone to do when he was edgy. She also saw the bailing twine they'd bound his wrists with was in two pieces at his feet. She hoped no one else had noticed that.

Hux dismounted, picked up her shotgun, opened the breach and unloaded the two barrels. With that, he nodded, and the other four men moved away and spread out around the property.

IT HAD BEEN NEARLY two hours since the strangers' search began—which had included the barn, Cotton's small cabin near the woods, the corral and bunkhouse, and the grounds inside the fence generally.

When two of the men came out of the house eating the jerky Luke had brought, Bran said, "Mama, they're taking—"

"Hush now."

Piper whispered, "Where's Luke?"

Virginia glanced at Hux, who'd stayed with them at the gate throughout, but the man was watching the others. She said, "He likely went home when he saw these men." She hoped he had.

Piper said, "Truly?"

Virginia nodded.

Bran tugged her sleeve. "Mama."

"What are they looking for?" Piper asked.

"*Piper...*"

"What if there's—"

"*Enough.*"

Bran said, "Mama, you said 'ain't' to that man. Grandpa always told us—"

"I know what your grandpa said. Now *shush it*! Both of you!"

Bran frowned. Which made Virginia want to reach for him. But she couldn't, couldn't face him now, either of them. She couldn't allow her children to see her tears. It was bad enough that the man at the gate could.

VIRGINIA STILL STOOD at the gate long after the men had left, long after she'd sent the children into the house. She was still standing there when the man named Cyrus reappeared on the far ridge, stopped, tipped his hat, and rode away again.

She looked down at her shotgun, which was open and empty where Hux had unloaded it. There was dirt and grass in the breach, which, even if she'd had the shells, rendered it useless.

What bothered her worse than that, however, worse than anything else, was the way the weapon trembled in her hands.

3

Sheriff Everett Reeves was feeling his age. He'd reached the stage of life where he found himself looking forward to simple comforts, like a good cup of coffee, a gentle breeze, and evenings with his wife Theresa—even when she went on and on about her flowers.

He'd heard older men talk of such things when he was still in his youth, remembered thinking them crazy or resigned to life—*dried up*. He'd even told one elderly gentleman that very thing back then, that for all intents and purposes the man was already dead.

But getting older wasn't so bad. Youth and all its ambitions and pursuits was tiring, and mostly fruitless anyway.

He sat back and swung his feet up on his desk. The position was comfortable but hard on his bony backside. He'd recently added a pillow to his ancient desk chair, which he'd inherited from his predecessor and swore was wrecking his back.

The pillow had been Theresa's idea. She'd come to his office, made all sorts of measurements, fussed over this, fussed over that, and then left with a determined look on her face. Ellis, his full-time deputy, had a different look on his face.

Everett told Ellis to go to hell. Ellis asked him where he thought they were presently stationed.

Everett had reluctantly gone along with it—the pillow —thinking the idea, at best, a stretch. He was also more than a little concerned about what it would look like to his critics, who were legion, it seemed.

But Theresa was right. She was always right. The cushion had helped with the pain, even relieved the queer tingling in his feet, so it was here to stay. Appearances be damned.

EVERETT RAISED his coffee to his lips and then promptly spilled it down his front when Deputy Ellis blasted through the door.

"Dammit, Ellis. Don't do that." The coffee wasn't hot anymore, but Everett knew it would take a minor miracle to get the stain out of his shirt.

"Sorry, Sheriff," Ellis said, half grinning. "You didn't get any on your cushion, did you?"

"Don't patronize me," the sheriff said. But he checked anyway.

Ellis said, "Somebody's hurt."

"Who?"

"Some stranger. Just rode into town."

Everett rolled his eyes. "Why are you telling me? Go find Dr. Holland."

"The guy's been shot."

"What do you mean?"

"Just that," Ellis said. "Some of his friends brought him into town a half hour ago with a gunshot wound."

"Where?"

"High in the chest or shoulder."

"No, I mean where did it happen? Who shot him?"

Ellis shrugged. "Don't know. His friends wouldn't let me question him, and they weren't volunteering anything. They even warned me off. And, Sheriff, when I tried to go past, I swear three of them started for their weapons."

"They threatened you?"

"Not in so many words, but they made it clear I wasn't welcome."

Everett lowered his feet and set the coffee cup on his desk. Folks getting emotional when a friend or loved one got hurt was common. He'd seen it plenty of times. Some would break down; some would commence blaming anyone in sight; some got protective. It was natural.

"You sure he was shot?" the sheriff asked.

"Saw him myself before they took him inside."

"How many are there?"

Ellis thought about it. "Three. Four, counting the one who's injured."

"And they're at Dr. Holland's place?"

"Yeah. They're even making Mrs. Holland stand outside. I tried to tell them she's his assistant, that she could help their friend, but they weren't having any of it."

"They're all armed?" Everett asked.

"To the teeth."

The sheriff shook his head. "Where's Donovan?"

"Probably working his place. He didn't come in today, what with nothing much going on."

Working his place, Everett thought. He hadn't seen hide nor hair of Donovan Odom since the part-time deputy had married Julie Breyer the month before. But that was probably how it ought to be.

"Go get him," Everett said.

Ellis nodded and headed for the door. "It's liable to take us a few minutes, Sheriff, so don't go inquiring of that bunch until we get back and ascertain their disposition." The deputy paused. "Besides, that pillow will likely go cold if you abandon it too long."

"Get out of my office, shitbird."

Ellis left laughing.

Everett shook his head as the door closed. He said, "You'll be old, too, someday."

THE TOWN of Cuttwood was average size, with all the same buildings and merchants every other place in this part of the country had. Its population didn't match, however. Hux had seen few people in the streets or stores as he rode in, which also could have meant Zalen and the other members of the group had arrived. They had that effect.

They had arrived. Hux found Zalen at a back table in the nearest tavern. He could also tell by the vacancy in the room, and the way the barkeep wouldn't make eye contact, that Zalen had been there a while.

Hux sat down across from him.

Zalen stirred the liquid in his cup, three swirls to the right, three swirls to the left, then took a sip. Hux didn't know what the concoction was—something of Zalen's own making, he figured—and he'd never asked.

Zalen set the cup on the table. "You spoke to her, Mr. Huxtable?"

"I didn't get a chance. They threw down on her before we could talk. They ..." Hux paused.

"You wish to add something?" Zalen asked.

"They were reckless," Hux said, "drunk on that reward you offered. It got them killed. It got Tess killed."

"Ah, yes—*the reward*. But that's precisely what's required to stimulate a desired behavior, Mr. Huxtable. Why else would creatures act in such a way that could cause them great harm?"

Hux didn't answer. It was dangerous to exchange too many words with Zalen.

Zalen said, "People recognize power and submit to it, because failure to do so causes them suffering and pain. But they are seldom proactive unless the end result produces a good in their lives they wouldn't otherwise have. *Incentive*, Mr. Huxtable. This is a thing you must learn."

Hux just nodded. In other words: Nobody in their right mind would've gone hunting for Tess unless there was a damned good reason—or they were crazy.

Hux let it go. Tess was never going to survive this thing anyway. Hux had known it; she had known it.

Zalen said, "Where is the rest of your party?"

Hux gestured toward the street outside. "Some of them brought Brady into town here to find a doctor. Ashe went with them. I sent the rest back to bury Sam and Tess. Figured they deserved it."

"No one deserves anything," Zalen said. "Anything else?"

Hux summarized their search of the Cooper place.

"What compelled you to stop there?" Zalen asked.

"Cyrus said he heard something in the woods near the area we found Sam and Tess. And that homestead was the only place around."

"And did you discover anything?"

"Nothing extraordinary. But it would help if I knew what I was looking for."

"You need assistance spotting the extraordinary?" Zalen asked.

Hux let out a breath. "I guess not."

Zalen sat back and closed his eyes. "First Eleanor, then Audrey, now Tess." His affinity for the women in the group was well known.

Eleanor had been caught by local authorities many years ago after a robbery gone bad. She'd escaped, Hux had been told, only to be recaptured, and then committed suicide in her jail cell. Apparently, that was the most remarkable thing about her—other than she was as crazy as a ten-legged spider.

Audrey, on the other hand, had been described by Zalen as the most efficient killer ever to rise from the animal kingdom, more lethal than any man he'd ever known. He'd compared her to some flower that disarmed its victims with the illusion of beauty and nectar, only to bleed them out when they least expected it and discard their bones like so much waste in a ditch. Those had been his words.

Hux hoped to never encounter such a flower.

Some of the senior members of the group had said

Audrey was worse than Zalen, more cold-blooded, brutal and cruel. Hux couldn't imagine such a thing. They'd said she'd been shot in the head after being cornered by a US marshal and his posse, that she'd killed as many as four of the marshal's men before going down.

But all that had been before Hux's time. He'd only been with the group a year or so, and he'd always figured the stories were stretched—which was often the case with tales of those who'd gone before, especially the dead ones.

There had been other women as well, but apparently none had left the legacy Eleanor and Audrey had, or Tess.

Except Moriya, who Zalen had recruited a couple of years ago when passing through Old Mexico. She was still crafting her legacy and was now the only woman left in the group. Moriya spoke little and preferred her privacy. And even Ashe gave her a wide berth when she entered the room. Randall had taken to calling her Winter—when she wasn't around, of course—because of the silence and cold that accompanied her presence. Hux didn't disagree.

Zalen said, "And Tess said nothing?"

"No."

"Who delivered the *coup de grâce*?"

"What's that?"

"Who finished her off?" Zalen said.

"Ashe. Even as I was calling for him to stop."

"Mr. Ashner isn't one for delay, is he?" Zalen said. Then: "A part of me wishes I could have been there."

"I think Tess wanted you there too."

Zalen grinned, leaned forward and stirred his drink. "Tell me about this woman at the ranch?"

"I don't think she knows anything."

"No, I mean what kind of woman is she?"

"She was ready to protect her children," Hux said, "but she was pretty shook up. She gave up her weapon."

Zalen frowned. "Typical."

"I think Cyrus wants to take a few boys and go back there."

"And I'm sure he will. His reward."

Hux shook his head. "Seems wrong."

"There is no wrong, Mr. Huxtable."

Hux looked up as Ashe pushed through the doors and started toward the table. Hux noticed the man had made no effort to stem the bleeding from his cheek.

Zalen said, "Why did she come here?"

"Tess?" Hux asked.

"Yes."

"Random," Hux said. "They just ran out of time and space. They were down to one horse."

Zalen glanced up at Ashe, who'd stopped beside him. Then, almost to himself, he said, "Tess never did anything randomly."

"The sheriff is coming," Ashe said.

"How much daylight is remaining?" Zalen asked.

"Enough."

"Are there any people on the street?"

"Some," Ashe said. "Not many."

Zalen finished his drink and stood. "Well, sometimes we must work with what we have."

EVERETT WAS on his way to Dr. Holland's place when the three men on horses swung into his path. He tipped his hat and tried to sidestep the riders, but they fanned out in front of him.

The man in the center of the trio said, "Everett Reeves, I am Zalen, and my companions here are called Ashe and Hux." He indicated the men on either side of him. "Let's make this brief, shall we?"

The man was hatless and had a sun-spotted shaved head.

Everett said, "You know my name, mister, but I don't believe we've met." He was sure they hadn't, sure he wouldn't have forgotten a fellow with a shaved head.

Zalen said, "We know many things, Sheriff, many things about your town. I also understand you have only two deputies, which is meager but also superfluous for such a diminutive settlement."

Everett looked at the one called Ashe. "The hell he just say?"

When Ashe remained silent, Everett said, "Y'all foreigners or something?"

"I'm here to request an update on the murder of my friends," Zalen said. "I want to know who you've brought to justice for their killings."

"I don't know nothing about any killings. Heard there's a wounded man with the doctor up the street. He with y'all?"

Zalen lowered his head. "Come now, Sheriff. Am I to believe you are unaware of the triple homicide within the boundaries of your jurisdictional responsibility?"

"What was that? That last part?"

"The area near that cliff and river where these obscene

slayings took place—that would be your jurisdiction, correct?"

"We cover what we can," Everett said. "But we can't be everywhere."

Zalen raised his head as Ellis and Donovan rounded the corner and stopped beside Everett. He said, "Ah, and there they are. We've been waiting for you, gentlemen."

Ellis and Donovan looked at Everett. Donovan said, "Sorry it took me so long, Sheriff."

Everett waved it off.

"Duty is everything to your constituency, Sheriff," Zalen went on. "Commitment. And in that regard, you have been found wanting."

Everett narrowed his eyes. "How's that?"

"You failed to protect my friends," Zalen said. "And you've allowed stolen property to circulate through your town."

Ellis stiffened. "Just a minute, now."

Everett placed a hand on his deputy's shoulder. "What's been stolen?"

Ignoring them both, Zalen said, "Therefore we've concluded that you've failed to discharge the duties of your office as a public servant. You have let down those entrusting you to protect them and their property. Do you know what that means, Everett? Do you understand what I'm telling you?"

Everett grinned and shook his head. He glanced at Ellis and rolled his eyes. "What're you telling me, mister?"

Zalen sat back in his saddle. "That actions have conse-quences, Sheriff. But so does inaction."

The man named Ashe raised his rifle.

Ellis said, "*Shit*!" and went for his pistol.

Everett threw up a hand. "Wait! What are you—"

Ashe shot Ellis in the chest before the deputy could lift his sidearm.

Donovan, who hadn't gone for his weapon, backpedaled and held up his hands defensively. "*No-no-no, please.*"

Ashe took careful aim before putting the second deputy down.

Everett screamed, "What the hell'd you do!" He dropped to his knees beside Ellis, who was still breathing, but coughing, and choking, and trying to speak.

Everett said, "What is it, son? What're you trying to say?"

Ellis said, "Tell—"

The next shot snapped Ellis's head back before he could finish.

Everett looked up, his right ear screaming from the close-range gunfire, and saw Ashe dismounted and aiming his rifle at him.

"You son of a bitch!" Everett screamed. He stood and faced Ashe.

Zalen said, "I'm willing to give you a second chance, Sheriff, an opportunity to redeem yourself."

"I'll see you rot in hell for this."

"Indeed," Zalen said," we will all rot at some point, won't we? But your journey doesn't have to end here. You and Theresa may continue what remains of your lives in peace, if you're willing to repent and take your duties seriously now."

"Don't speak my wife's name, you coward." Everett said. "Come down from that mount and settle this."

"I imagine Theresa will be disappointed by your decision."

"My wife has nothing to do with this. You and me are—"

"Ah, but your fates are entwined," Zalen said. "Are they not? You are *one*, aren't you? The mystery of the marriage union?"

"The hell you talking about?"

"Simple," Zalen said. "The choices you make directly affect Theresa as well as yourself. Marriage. Your actions, her consequences, and vice-versa. And, dear Everett, I should pass along a message now, lest I forget: Theresa begs you to choose wisely."

Everett felt the ground shift beneath him. He fell back a step, nearly tripped over Donovan's body, and looked around the abandoned town center. Both sides of the street were lined with armed men now, all having seemingly appeared from nowhere, all hooded beneath burlap sacks.

"Theresa!"

"Oh, no, Sheriff, we would not hold her nearby."

Everett rushed over to Zalen's horse. "Wait. Where is she? She's not well. You can't keep her—"

Zalen looked down at the sheriff's hand on his sleeve. "Not even a minute has passed and already you have shown poor judgement."

Everett removed his hand.

"And one judgement leads to another," Zalen said. "Inevitability, right?"

"What?"

"That decision"—Zalen gestured at his sleeve—"will cost your wife three fingers. You might've used four, but let us go with three."

"Wait, I didn't—"

"And because I'm feeling magnanimous," Zalen went on, "and perhaps because you didn't fully comprehend the guidelines, I'm going to let you choose: fingers or toes?"

"Please don't do this," Everett said. "Please, I'm begging you."

"Which will it be?"

"I can't ... Please, I didn't—"

"I can select for you, if you wish," Zalen said.

"What do you want? Just tell me what you want?"

"Fingers it is, then."

Everett crumpled to the ground, began to weep. "*Toes.*"

Zalen turned his horse. "Find my missing property, Sheriff, and then you may return to the comfort of your wife and chair."

Everett said, "Wait. What did you lose?"

"Be imaginative, Sheriff," Zalen said. "Be creative. Investigate. I assure you; it isn't difficult." Then: "Oh, yes, for the sake of clarity, if you speak of our agreement to anyone, or attempt to send for outside help, we will consider that an ill-advised use of your tongue, just like with your fingers a moment ago. Theresa would probably be *very* disappointed if you made that mistake."

Everett felt like he was going to be sick.

Zalen said, "But, hey, she wouldn't be able to tell you about it, would she?" He laughed. "Most husbands wouldn't mind that, huh, Sheriff?"

• • •

Hux watched the defeated old man sobbing in the street, watched as he alternately looked at his hands, his deputies, his hands. Hux listened as the sheriff spoke their names, and then his wife's, over and over, again and again.

Zalen said, "*Incentive*, Mr. Huxtable. Do you understand?"

Hux nodded.

"You will ensure the good sheriff's wife receives his selection?"

"Yes."

"Be prompt," Zalen said. Then he turned and laid the back of his hand on Ashe's wounded cheek. He said, "*Tess*."

4

——————

Except for the few minutes she'd sneaked away from her chores to inspect the strange object she'd found the day before, Piper had been watching her mom most of the day.

Her mom and Cotton had been working on the stump near the front gate. Which was weird because the stump didn't need to be worked on, didn't need to be removed. Her mom had told Piper that herself. But there they'd been, Mom and Cotton, shovels, picks, and saws, longer than half the day now.

Piper had hoped to explore her discovery the night before, had been giddy at the prospect of it. But her mom had been up more than half the night, sitting at the table, staring at the same spot on the wall, and Piper had been too tired to wait her out.

The thing turned out to be a crumpled piece of paper tied around an ordinary dirty rock, which was a letdown of the highest sort. Worse still, Piper couldn't even read the writing on the paper, which was mostly composed of the letters she recognized, but all seeming in the wrong order. It looked like something Cotton would write, if he could write.

When Bran had come barreling into the room a moment later—"You've gotta work too!"—she had wrapped the page back around the rock and slipped it into her drawer before he could see.

She had thought of telling her mom about the mysterious paper, even considered taking it out to the old stump to show it to her. But her mom had seemed someplace else for the last full day, and she'd become edgy and short anytime Piper asked her a question, which was also weird. Did she know she and Bran had left their chores to play by the river the day before?

As Cotton walked away with the tools, Virginia finished cinching up her packs and tightening the straps on her saddle.

The two men had first appeared at daybreak, positioned on the same ridge north of the house, just silhouettes in the struggling early sun. But even at a distance Virginia had known who they were. What she hadn't known was how long they'd been there.

The second time she'd seen them was less than an hour ago, and they were closer this time—not close enough to speak or communicate, but close enough to see clearly. The same two from yesterday—the blond and the one called Cyrus.

Virginia had pretended not to notice them. The men had shown no such pretense.

"Where are you going, Mama?"

Virginia flinched at the sound of Piper's voice. How long had she been standing there? Virginia turned back to her gelding. "Town."

"This late?"

"Got business with the sheriff."

"Can I come?"

"Not this time."

"But it'll be dark before you get back."

"Dark never hurt no one."

"Is it because of those men?" Piper asked.

"That ain't none of your affair."

"What did they want?"

"I suspect they were just passing through. Folks do that."

Piper was quiet a moment. Then: "What if they come back while you're gone?"

Virginia had thought about that too. Her place was flanked by the river to the north and west and there was only one easy way across it—a bridge built hastily during the war. So unless the men had circled back around to the south, which made no sense, she'd likely encounter them on her way into Cuttwood and still have time to double back if she had to. But once she crossed the river …

"Mama?"

"They won't," Virginia said. "But if they do, you and Bran take to the woods down in the bottomlands. You know where I'm talking about?"

"Yeah, but that's where Cotton likes to go."

"That's right. The thicket is plentiful down there, lots of places for you two to hole up."

Piper looked toward the lower portion of the property.

"They won't come back," Virginia said. "They got no cause to."

"What about Cotton?"

"He'll probably go down there with you. Tell him to show you a good place to hunker down."

"He makes me edgy."

"Baby, Cotton's no threat to anyone."

"But how do you know?" Piper said. "He don't even talk."

"Your grandpa put him on years ago. If he trusted him, that ought to ease your mind."

Virginia could tell it didn't.

"I don't like the way he looks at me," Piper said.

Virginia sighed. She wondered about that too. Cotton was a man, after all. Her father had speculated that Cotton's family had died or been killed when he was young, that he'd been shuffled around ever since. How her father had concluded this, Virginia didn't know. Querying Cotton wouldn't help either. She'd tried that, but she'd never been able to get more than two words from the man. She felt like her daughter resented her for keeping him around.

"If you're concerned about those men," Piper said, "why not bring Deputy Ellis back with you? He can stay in the bunkhouse. I can get it ready for him while you're gone."

The idea had crossed Virginia's mind. Ellis was a sweet man, always bringing Piper a flower and Bran a coin when he "*just happened to be in the area.*" That was his nature. Of course, Virginia knew what else he was thinking. He'd once told her, in his own passive sort of way, that a man was a necessary component on a ranch this size.

Still, Virginia wasn't completely against the notion, and Ellis had always offered her help.

Piper backed away as Virginia swung into the saddle. "When will you be back?"

Virginia glanced toward the empty ridge to the north. "Double quick. You'll not even know I'm gone."

Piper frowned and started back to the house.

As she rode away, Virginia saw Cotton settle down on the porch and begin carving. She also saw Piper watching her from the window.

"SHALL WE BEGIN?" Zalen asked.

Hux nodded, and though he'd never admit it, he'd felt a wash of relief when Zalen suggested they start their search outside of town.

They'd been in the tavern all day, sitting at the same table in the back, having the same conversations Zalen like to have—namely, one-sided.

Hux had stopped looking over his shoulder hours ago, stopped closing his eyes or lowering his head. But he'd only recently stopped flinching at the sound of the gunshots, screams, and cries for help outside.

The day had been long and, for Hux, mostly uneventful. The group, however, was having their way with the little town of Cuttwood. *Their reward*, as Zalen put it, would generally last the entire day and sometimes longer depending on the objective they'd completed.

Zalen had moved from his seat only once, and only

when a member of the group leaned through the door and insisted he see something.

Hux had followed Zalen outside onto the boardwalk in time to see an older man with a long white beard charging up the street, shotgun in hand, streaks of tears on his cheeks.

The man was screaming, "Let the coward come out!" over and over again.

Hux learned afterward that the man was an ex-US marshal and war veteran. He was also the father of the deputy named Ellis.

Ashe leaned his rifle against a hitching post and met the man halfway up the street.

When the man noticed Ashe advancing toward him, he said, "Arm yourself, stranger."

When Ashe only kept coming, the man raised his weapon and fired, and Hux saw Ashe's right arm tug back.

But Ashe never missed a stride, eventually snatching the shotgun from the old man's hands and proceeding to beat him with it mercilessly.

Hux had never seen anything like it, not even during his brief stint in the military, not even amidst the carnage of the Indian Wars.

He had turned away after the stock of the weapon broke and shattered against the old man's head.

The deputy's father was still lying in the street as Hux and Zalen saddled their mounts and rode out of town. He wasn't moving, wasn't moaning, wasn't asking for help. And, Hux knew, he would never do any of those things again.

· · ·

Julie Odom was sitting on the floor when someone began knocking on the door.

Why couldn't she stop shaking?

She'd been wondering what she was going to do, praying for guidance, questioning that guidance. But most of all, she'd been regretting not telling Donovan she was pregnant.

She'd waited up half the night for her husband, even considered riding into town during the small hours of dark but didn't because she knew that would upset him. Never did she imagine him dead.

He couldn't be dead.

The knocking changed to a deep, insistent *thump-thump-thump*, like someone was striking the door with the heel of their hand. She glanced at the darkening window near the rear of the house. What time was it?

The sheriff had come by early in the morning after Donovan failed to return home, and she'd been on the floor ever since.

"I'm sorry, Julie. I'm just so damn sorry."

The terrible, continuous echoes of Everett's voice brought wave upon wave of fresh, raw pain, and kept alive the awful twisting and burning in her throat and guts.

The sheriff had asked her questions as well: if she'd come across anything that didn't belong to her, if she knew where his wife was—each inquiry bringing new tears, each one pushing her to the brink of screaming.

There was more, but she couldn't remember it, couldn't make sense of what she did remember. When she began rocking and yelling and pulling her hair, the sheriff had touched her shoulder and said something about coming back later.

There was nothing after that, nothing but the lingering scent of her husband filling the house, and here and there, his soft, disembodied whispers from across the room.

She never heard Everett leave.

Thump-thump-thump ...

HUX STEPPED BACK when the door opened.

Zalen said, "You are Mrs. Julie Odom, correct?"

The young woman nodded. "Do I know you, mister?"

"I wish to offer my condolences for the loss of your husband."

The woman wiped her eyes and bit her bottom lip. She held the door open and Hux removed his hat and followed Zalen inside.

Zalen stopped in the middle of the room and completed a full turn, taking in the house—a small place, still partially under construction, cozy.

Julie Odom said, "You knew my Donovan?"

Still looking around, Zalen said, "To claim to know someone seems an intensely personal thing, wouldn't you agree? Truth is, I was only briefly acquainted with your late husband. But I saw the last look on his face, Mrs. Odom, and I wish to report that I believe his final thoughts were about you."

Julie brushed away tears. "You were there?"

"Indeed I was, Mrs. Odom. I'm the one who had him killed."

Julie swayed on her feet, reached for support that wasn't there.

Zalen said, "And I regret to inform you that your husband was a coward of the most pathetic sort. Why, he was begging like a child before my associate gunned him down."

Julie said, "But ... but, *why*?"

"My property and my friends. Your husband failed in his duty to protect them on my behalf, on your little township's behalf. I was doing your community a favor."

Julie blinked and looked around the room uncomprehendingly. Then her eyes flared and snapped back to Zalen. She thrust a finger toward the door. "Get out of my house!"

Zalen backhanded her, and she twisted around and dropped to her knees. He dragged a chair next to her and sat down. "You will lower your head when you speak to me, Mrs. Odom. And you will never raise your voice in my presence."

Julie touched her cheek.

"Do you understand?" Zalen asked.

She nodded.

Zalen sat back. "I am not here because I believe you have my property. But my comrade is going to search your place nonetheless—you and I both know how husbands sometimes keep things from their wives. And while he looks around, you are going to prepare a meal for us."

Julie said nothing.

"What will you be serving us tonight?" Zalen asked.

Julie's eyes remained on the floor. She shook her head.

Zalen slapped her again and she crumpled and rolled onto her side.

Hux saw a string of blood connecting from the floor to the tip of her nose. He also saw her reach for her stomach.

"You will respond promptly when I speak to you," Zalen said.

"There's back strap," Julie said in a hoarse whisper, "and bacon, I think."

Zalen rubbed his hands together. "I have always been enchanted by the smell of bacon. Tell me, what type of back strap do you speak of?"

"Venison."

"Ah, yes," Zalen said. "Also a delicacy." He looked at Hux. "Shall we have both?"

"That'd be fine," Hux said.

"Indeed," Zalen said. "I'm sure it will be. And, Mrs. Odom, I also expect you to locate and return my property within the next two days. Failure to do so will result in a second visit to your charming little cottage here." He leaned down and spoke into her ear. "And you should know, dear lady, most folks find the second visit quite unpleasant. Do you understand?"

She nodded.

"Wonderful," Zalen said. "Now, shall we have that generous supper you offered?"

As Julie Odom struggled to her feet and moved toward the cookware, Zalen turned to Hux. "We will begin our search in earnest tomorrow, after our associates have fully absorbed their reward. And I feel obliged to prepare you, Mr. Huxtable, this being your first experience with such measures, the people of this town will likely begin to hate us then."

5

Virginia started feeling anxious after crossing the bridge. So far, she hadn't seen any evidence of the two men, no tracks or voices, no shapes on the horizon. But she found that fact somehow more unsettling.

The bridge, of course, wasn't the only way across the river. There were a handful of areas where a determined person and a strong-minded horse could reach the other side. For a non-local, those places would take some time to locate, but they were there. And her babies were on the other side.

She glanced at her shotgun, which was secured in a saddle boot. She hadn't fired the weapon since Piper was little and felt less than confident the old thing would work.

Still, the piece brought a measure of comfort she knew she wouldn't otherwise have, and even if a false assurance, she was grateful for whatever she could get.

. . .

BEFORE THE FAMILIAR contours of Cuttwood were fully visible in the failing light, Virginia thought she heard a scream. Three gunshots followed, then nothing.

The sounds gave her pause because she was sure they'd come from the direction of town. But all was quiet when she steered her mount between the first few buildings of the commerce section. Too quiet, in fact. She didn't even see anyone on the boardwalk, which was normally a popular haunt at this time of day. The whole place had an unnatural quality about it, like the guilty when trying too hard to hide something.

BRADY MOVED AWAY from the window and walked back to the bar. He nudged Chester.

Chester jerked his blade and whirled around, giving Brady only a second to jump back and avoid the tip of his knife.

Even so, the blade's edge brushed against his shirt, much closer than he liked or expected, leaving his heart racing and beads of sweat forming on his brow.

He'd been lucky, he knew, partly because he'd anticipated the reaction, mostly because Chester was drunk.

There was never a good time to interrupt Chester, but it was especially dangerous when he'd been sitting alone for hours with a bottle and that empty dead glare in his eyes.

Chester had stabbed a man years before under similar circumstances, an unsuspecting cowboy who'd touched his shoulder while Chester was submerged in one of his whiskey-soaked reveries. The cowboy had died in misery a day later. And all because, or so Brady had heard, he'd wanted to know if the seat next to Chester was taken.

There had been others since that unfortunate cowboy back west—two more today, in fact. Like many, Chester had come through the war a different person—or, as some had said, no longer a person at all. Most agreed it was only a matter of time before he turned his rifle, or that hideous knife, on himself.

"It's me, man," Brady said.

Chester grunted and sheathed his blade, but not before the void pulsated like a heartbeat in his eyes. Brady hated being on the receiving end of Chester's black stares. It always looked like he was making some awful decision, and nothing turned Brady's system to liquid faster.

Brady gestured at the window. "I figure there's something you'd like to see."

As Brady moved aside to allow room for the man's considerable bulk, he accidentally bumped into the wall behind him.

Brady cringed and moaned and blinked away tears. He swore under his breath. The pain in his shoulder was like a white-hot stab from the devil himself, so intense that it sometimes blurred his vision and moved the ground beneath his feet.

It had also prevented him from fully taking part with the others in the group today.

"*Damn you, Tess.*"

The whiskey had taken the edge off the wound, which turned out to be a clean in-and-out, little more than a graze—or so said the doctor. Even so, Brady knew there'd be hell to pay when the sun rose and he sobered up.

But that was tomorrow.

He tapped on the window, and Chester looked out at the abandoned street.

Brady pointed at the horse tied in front of the sheriff's office.

Chester looked at him. "The hell I care about a horse?"

Brady had watched the woman come into town, watched her hitch her mount and push through the doors of the sheriff's office.

She was lean and sinewy, hair pulled tight against her scalp and tied off at the back. And even in the dark, he could see she had the same hardened look that most in this part of the country possessed. At the same time, she had a graceful motion about her, a movement that reminded Brady of flowing water or fine music.

After describing this to Chester, Brady said, "There's a shed behind that livery stable across the way. She'll have to pass by it on her way out."

Chester looked back out the window. The expression on his face chilled Brady to the marrow, and for a moment he almost felt sorry for the woman.

SHERIFF REEVES WAS SLUMPED OVER, head on his desk. His hat was on the floor at his feet and a half empty glass of amber liquid stood next to his inert hand.

Virginia said, "Everett?"

The sheriff jerked up. He recoiled in his chair and held out a hand, eyes darting around the room.

Virginia looked around too. For what? She didn't know.

Everett eventually lowered his hand and reached for the glass, but apparently changed his mind. As if just noticing her, he said, "Good lord, Virginia, you shouldn't be here."

"What do you mean?"

"I mean you shouldn't be here. Why would you come into town now?"

"There's been some strange men about my place over the past day and a half. I figured you'd—"

The sheriff let out a laugh, ran a hand over his face.

"What?" Virginia asked.

"You're late to the dance, girl."

"Say again?"

The sheriff produced a handkerchief and held it against his head, grimaced as if struck by a sudden pain.

"Talk to me, Everett."

"They're here, too, Virginia, more of them than I can count. They said they'll be going through our homes in the morning and there ain't no one to stop them. They've," he paused, "they've already killed six people that I know of."

"Where's Ellis?"

"Oh, Virginia, you've got to get out of here, just get out of here now."

"Where's Ellis?"

"He's dead, dammit! Him and Donovan both."

Virginia placed a hand against the wall.

"You've got to get out of here," the sheriff said again, "and I mean out of the territory. They'll be spreading out and it's only a matter of time before they make it to your place."

"What do they want?"

The sheriff shook his head and stared at his hands.

"Everett?"

"What?"

"Those men. What do they—"

The sheriff suddenly leaned forward. "You've got to check your place, search for anything that don't belong."

"Like what?"

"Anything! Dig, lift floorboards, search the woods. Leave anything you find on the porch and I'll fetch it after you leave."

Virginia said nothing.

"Are you armed?" the sheriff asked.

"Shotgun on the horse."

"Lord in heaven, woman." He opened a drawer, withdrew a revolver and held it out to her.

Virginia shook her head. "I don't like those things."

Everett flung the pistol at her. "Haven't you been listening!"

Virginia moved aside just before the revolver would've caught her in the midsection. The piece hit the floor, spun, slid, and settled in the corner.

"They'll kill you," Everett said. "Don't you understand? You're on your own. I can't help you. And God only knows what they'll do to your children."

"Have you sent word to Marshal Perkins?"

Everett jumped to his feet. "Don't you dare!"

Virginia fell back a step.

But the sheriff seemed lost again. He stood motionless, finger and eyes pointing at her, but his mind somewhere else. "Don't you interfere with me," he said finally, and his voice didn't sound like his own.

"I wouldn't, Everett."

"See to it that you don't," he said. And when he sat back down and reached for the glass, Virginia thought she saw tears.

She moved to leave.

"Virginia."

She looked back, hand on the door.

"Have you seen my Theresa?"

"I came straight here. Ain't she home?"

Everett didn't answer.

"Everett?"

The sheriff looked away. "Go on, woman."

BRADY PEERED around the edge of the livery stable. "She'll be coming now."

He'd already seen the woman mount her horse, turn it, then pause and look back at the sheriff's office.

She'd finally kicked the horse into a swift lope. And she'd no doubt be coming fast, which complicated things—for her. Removing someone from a fast-moving horse wasn't hard if one knew what they were doing.

And Chester did. He would swing the stock of his rifle high and catch her in the face. It was a difficult maneuver, but a blow to the gut wouldn't guarantee a clean and immediate dismount like a shot to the mouth would.

It was also an awful thing to see. Often the worst part for the victim. Instantly disabling. Sometimes permanently.

Excitement washed through Brady, a cool tingle in his neck and shoulders. The thrill of the hunt. The anticipation of conquest.

She was near enough now to see, to smell, to taste. His senses were alive and raw, hungry.

And then the hair on the back of his neck prickled. That heretofore pleasant stream of energy tightened into knots in his back and chest, turned cold.

He slipped back a step, narrowed his eyes and looked down.

Chester must have sensed it as well, because he suddenly dropped his rifle and spun, his blade already in his hand.

The shape behind them moved, too, sidestepped, caught Chester's hand and turned the knife back into the big man's chest. Chester let go and fell against the wall. The shape tapped him three times above his collar, fist closed around the blade—*pat-pat-pat.* Chester slumped to the ground, gagging and trying to stop the flow of blood from his throat.

Brady drew his sidearm and fired wildly with his good arm, but the dark figure swatted his pistol away and pressed the crimson point of Chester's knife under his chin.

Brady tried to scramble back but only met the side of the livery stable. "Wait! For God's sake, just wait! You have no idea what you're doing, mister."

The man leaned close, face obscured below the brim of his hat and the shade of night. He said, "I'm looking for Mason."

6
_____

Virginia watched Luke cross the front of the property on his way to the barn where Piper and Bran were.

He was early today. And while he tipped his hat as he passed, he didn't stop to speak with her, nor did he close the gate. Which was strange.

The early sun harassed Virginia's eyes and mind and was quickly contributing to a terrible headache. The ability to go without sleep had served her well in the past, had given her that edge she often needed. But her body wasn't the same anymore. Time and children and the land in general had seen to that.

She turned to Cotton, who was sitting beside her on the porch. "Please close the gate."

Cotton got up and set his carving knife and wood on his chair. Virginia picked up his latest creation—a timber wolf standing in profile, its head angled to the left as if something had grabbed its attention. The likeness was remarkable, perfectly proportioned from the dimensions of its legs, head, and tail to the slight rise of its hackles. The piece was so exact in its resemblance that Virginia wondered if the big man was working from a particular memory.

Cotton didn't meet her eyes when he returned—he seldom did—but just looked at her hands. When Virginia offered the wolf and knife back, he took them quickly, careful not to touch her.

"I like this one," she said. "Did you see this wolf?"

"Yes'um."

"Whereabouts?"

Cotton looked toward the woods to the west.

Virginia said, "Has it come near the stock?"

Cotton didn't answer.

It was exceedingly uncommon to see a timber wolf anymore, and rarer still for one to appear and stir up livestock. But it did happen. And Virginia could ill afford any more losses among the animals.

"What about those two men?" she asked. "You seen them this morning?"

Cotton glanced at the ridge to the north. "Yes'um."

VIRGINIA HAD FELT uneasy when leaving Cuttwood the night before, resisting the urge to spur her horse into a run even while still navigating the final bends of town.

Though she'd wanted to get home with all possible speed, she'd been mindful of her animal's endurance at that point, concerned over tiring it too quickly.

All that changed when she'd heard the gunshot, which sounded like it had come from directly behind her. She even thought she saw it, a quick flash of light in the otherwise dark landscape.

She'd spun around in the saddle, expecting to see someone bearing down on her, but there was only the same narrow street behind her, dark, quiet, and vacant.

Nevertheless, she'd leaned against the pommel and whipped her gelding into a gallop. She never spotted any pursuers, nor any sign of the two watchers on her way back.

She'd also dismissed any worry over her horse's stamina.

The sheriff had made little sense, but what he'd said had been enough. The rest of it was easy to piece together on her own.

She'd been surprised at how powerfully the news of Ellis's death had affected her. She was taken aback at how, given everything Everett had told her, the loss of the deputy dominated her thinking.

She had learned years ago to avoid attachment. She'd been told such things were under her control, that she had the power to choose where to place her emotions. She'd believed it, practiced it, thought she'd mastered the discipline. But she'd been wrong.

It hadn't been like Landry, whose looks, charm, and promises had washed over her like a cool northwestern breeze when she was young. She had opened herself to Landry in ways she'd be wary to admit now, even with her children, *his* children, ways that embarrassed her still.

But it wasn't that way with Ellis, never had been. In fact, she hadn't known she cared for the deputy until last night, hadn't known she was still capable of caring.

Piper and Bran—she'd left no room for anyone or

anything else. Her children were her breath, her life, the blood in her veins. Every decision she'd made since Piper was small had been for the good of her babies, to keep them safe, to show them a world different from the one she'd known.

She heard Everett's words: *They'll kill you ... You're on your own.*

She saw Piper greet Luke at the front of the barn and tug him around to the back. This was the only place Piper had ever known, or at least remembered. Her daughter still spoke wistfully of playing with Grandpa in the yard, the challenges he'd create for her and Bran—the first to catch an ornery chicken, who could ride the crankiest pig the longest. He'd called it Cooper's barnyard rodeo and even fabricated ribbons for the champions. Piper still had one. So did Bran.

Everett again: *God only knows what they'll do to your children.*

Piper and Bran had been lost after Virginia's father died. Virginia had seen them both standing alone in the yard from time to time since then, revisiting, what was for them, old memories, good memories.

There had been the frowns and tears that seemed to strike from nowhere, but there had also been the eventual steps forward, the new games and challenges, the discoveries of their own imaginations. In a sense, Virginia knew, as long as they still tread the same ground, their grandpa was still with them.

Dad.

Virginia wiped her eyes, surprised that she needed to, and then turned to Cotton. "What would you do?"

Cotton went on carving, said nothing.

"I THOUGHT you was supposed to be smart," Piper said, "you having a teacher for a father and all."

"He's not been a professor for a long time." Luke adjusted his spectacles as he studied the paper. "And what's being smart got to do with deciphering gibberish?"

"What's gibberish? A bird or something?"

Luke laughed.

Piper said, "What?"

"You."

"What about me?"

"A *bird*, Piper?"

She'd brought the mysterious page out to the barn hoping that Luke could make sense of it. She'd been delighted when he arrived early and had immediately taken him around the back for privacy—which with Bran around was a forlorn hope. Her younger brother had already peered around the corner twice, the first time to make the *shame-shame* gesture with his fingers, the second time to throw a rock at her.

"So what's it say?" she asked.

"It doesn't say anything," Luke said. "It just looks like random letters to me. Where'd you find it?"

Piper told him.

Luke frowned.

"What?" Piper asked.

He touched her chin. "Just put it away and we'll work on it when I get back."

"Get back? Where are you going?"

"I've got to run an errand for Father. It'll only take a couple of days."

"A couple of days?" Piper said. "What've you got to do?"

"Nothing special, just an errand. Nothing like we'll do when we're married."

Piper felt herself flush. "What makes you think I'll marry a ranch hand?"

He shrugged and turned to leave.

Piper said, "What would we do?"

Luke looked over his shoulder, grinning. "It's a secret. I want to surprise you ... I mean, my future wife, whoever that might be."

She smacked his arm. "You'll hurry back?"

"Quick as I can."

"'Cause somebody's got to do your chores, you know."

BRADY FINGERED the puncture wound in his neck, same as he'd been doing for the last half-hour—his neck or injured shoulder.

"Just one drink?" he said. "To take the edge off, you know?"

Zalen said, "Do not ask that again."

"Okay, Zee."

"Were you inebriated last night?"

"Huh?"

"Had you been drinking?"

"Yeah, we'd had a few, but I still had my wits."

Moriya drifted in from the side door of the tavern and leaned against the wall.

Hux watched her as she entered, as did everyone else. She was small and thin like a bird, and a snake. Her fierce dark eyes flicked from one person to the next until she'd taken in the whole room, and then they settled on Hux.

Hux looked away.

Zalen said, "I find it extraordinary that one man was able to incapacitate Chester so easily."

"He snuck up on us," Brady said. "He's a cowardly bastard."

"Plenty of men have attempted to sneak up on Chester," Zalen said. "And, dear Brady, Chester wasn't killed from behind. So far as I can ascertain, he was stabbed a total of four times in the chest and neck, and with his own blade, I should add."

"The guy took it from him. Chester turned around and the guy just took it."

Zalen said, "Did he ride up behind you, run in from the countryside, or just rise up from the dust of the earth itself?"

Brady ran a hand over his face. "Like I said, he was just there. I kind of *felt* him, you know, and then he was behind us. I think Chester did too."

"Did what?"

"Felt him."

Zalen shook his head.

"Honest, Zee. That's how it was."

"What else did he say?" Hux asked.

"Nothing, man. He just said he was looking for Mason, said it twice. The second time's when he nearly put Chester's blade through my neck." Brady touched his throat again. "I thought I was a dead man."

"Mason who?"

"I don't know. I asked him the same thing. I don't know any Masons and I told him so."

"What did he do then?"

"Nothing. He just backed away and disappeared like ..." Brady looked at the table.

"Like what?" Hux asked.

"Like a ghost."

Moriya said something in Spanish, then turned and slipped through the door to the street.

Zalen frowned and glanced back at her, a thoughtful but incredulous look on his face. He was quiet a moment, watching as the door settled after her. Then he slid back from the table and approached the woman behind the bar.

The Indian woman possessed the same piercing dark stare as Moriya, only a few degrees warmer.

"And what is your name?" Zalen asked.

The woman's eyes moved from Hux to Zalen. "I am Sally White Horse."

Zalen slapped her. "You will lower your head when you speak to me."

She did.

"First," Zalen said, "I must know: how does one of your kind find herself keeping bar?"

"Ham Greenly. He take me in when my parents killed."

"So you are Mrs. Greenly?"

"I am Sally White Horse."

"How fascinating," Zalen said. "I must speak with this Mr. Greenly. I must hear the story."

She looked up at him. "Your man kill him last night."

Zalen slapped her again, a vicious blow, and Hux saw two scarlet lines begin creeping down her chin.

Sally White Horse lowered her head but made no move to wipe the blood away.

Zalen said, "My associate tells me you saw the man who did this."

"I saw him."

"He came in here?"

"He come here."

"Who was he?" Zalen asked.

"I do not know this man."

"But he is from your quaint little town, correct?"

"I have never seen this man."

"Tell me, then," Zalen said, "how do you know he's the one who killed our friend?"

"I see it in his face. Your man talk loud. He hear them."

"What did he say to you—this man?"

"He ask for water."

Zalen chuckled. "He requested water from a barkeep?"

"He ask for water."

"Anything else?"

"He want Mason."

"And what did you say?"

"I do not know Mason."

"What did he look like?" Hux asked.

She waved a hand to include all the men in the room. "He look like you; except he no hide under a sack."

Zalen reached across the bar and touched her bloody chin. "Your spirit calls to me, little one. It is an uncommon quality you possess. Under different circumstances ..." He paused, thought about something, then finally said, "Pity," and nodded to Ashe.

As Zalen turned to leave, she raised her head. "He do right. He hear your man talk, talk about what they will do to the woman, and he do right."

Zalen pushed through the door without looking back.

ASHE DRAGGED Sally White Horse across the street and pinned her against the wall of the dry goods store. He checked her for weapons, forced her to her knees, then snapped his fingers and Brady stumbled over.

Brady drew his pistol and held it against the side of her head.

Zalen moved to the center of the street and raised his voice to the town, though most of its occupants were in hiding now. "This is the consequences of interference," he said. "A life for a life. You remove one of ours, and we remove one of yours. And if this happens again, we will remove two of yours, then three, until none is left among you."

The group members appeared and lined one side of the street, all hooded beneath the burlap sacks, all behind Zalen.

Zalen said, "Let the one who slithers under the blanket of night come forth and offer himself as a sacrifice for those of you he has transgressed. If he shows courage and fortitude, if he atones for his trespass, this season will pass you by. If he remains in the shadows, however, this, dear Cuttwood, is what you will become acquainted with."

Zalen raised a hand and signaled behind him.

Everyone turned toward Sally White Horse, simultaneously bracing for the report from Brady's pistol.

But Sally White Horse wasn't there. Only Brady remained against the wall of the dry goods store, slumped down, head forward. The handle of Chester's knife was sticking out of his chest.

7

Virginia tripped and nearly fell down the steps as she heard Cotton opening the gate outside.

She had snapped awake at the table when the rusty hinges whined out front and then bolted for the door when she couldn't make out anything through the evening window.

She reached her old friend just in time to help him down from his horse. "Ephraim, what on earth—"

"*Shhhh* …" The old man patted her shoulder. "Let us not start that."

Ephraim looked like someone stepping onto the dock after a long and tiring journey at sea, and Virginia had to give him a moment to settle his feet.

"What are you doing here?" she asked. "You shouldn't—"

Ephraim clasped her face between his hands. "My girl, you look so tired. You know how that concerns me."

"Heaven's mercy, Ephraim, why are you alone? Where's Luke?"

Ephraim tilted his chin back and drank in the air like it was a delicacy. "What's left of a man if he can't saddle his horse and enjoy a fine evening's ride? What's left of his life?"

Virginia shook her head.

Piper and Bran hurried up from the lower portion of the property, all smiles and jitters at the sight of Ephraim.

Virginia whirled on them. "Where have you been?" she snapped. "I told you to stay in the house!"

Piper just looked at her.

Bran said, "You didn't tell us that, Mama."

Ephraim stepped between them and began handing out his special pastries to Piper and Bran. He also passed two solid blocks of aspen wood to Cotton—the big man's favorite timber to carve—who took them and turned away without a word.

Virginia started to speak, but Ephraim returned to his packs and filled her arms with three cuts of pork and several loaves of bread.

"From our latest slaughter," he said. "Shall we make an evening of it?"

Virginia had to help Ephraim up the steps, which bothered her deeply. Ephraim had been her father's best friend and, consequently, like an uncle to her. He and her father had both given up jobs as educators to travel to the frontier—which they'd viewed as liberation, Virginia had been told. But it turned out to be nothing of the sort.

Ephraim had lost his wife Janie to Luke's unexpected arrival, and later his barn and half his crop to fire.

Janie had been more than twenty-five years her husband's junior and her death had shocked everyone. In the years following—aside from finding relief in Luke, and later Virginia's own children—Ephraim had never been the same. He'd once confided to Virginia that he'd never forgiven himself for not taking Janie into the city for help with the delivery, and he didn't think his Creator would either.

Ephraim pushed his plate away, grinned at Virginia and rubbed his stomach.

Virginia said, "Thanks for this."

"Thank you, my girl."

"You'll stay with us tonight."

Ephraim shook his head. "Not this time." He leaned close to Virginia and angled his head away from the children, who were just finishing their meals. "I expect you know why I'm here."

"I reckon I do."

"They've taken over Cuttwood."

"I heard."

"And they've been through here too. Isn't that right?"

Virginia nodded.

Ephraim said, "Do you know what they're doing to the townspeople?"

"I can only imagine."

"It's worse than you think, Virginia. And I'm told there's more than twenty of them."

Virginia closed her eyes.

"What are you planning to do?" Ephraim asked.

Virginia stood and collected the empty plates. She placed them on the counter and, though it was full dark now, stared out the window for a time.

She'd left the day's work with Cotton while she sat at the table and contemplated that very question. But no easy answers were forthcoming; they never were.

She said, "I'm going to do what I do."

She looked at Ephraim and he looked at her.

Ephraim glanced at Piper and Bran, who'd gotten up and become occupied with something in the corner of the room. He said, "You can't, Virginia."

"Can't pack up and run."

"Yes you can. Luke says your aunt has offered you refuge back east. He wasn't gossiping; he's just afraid you'll take Piper away."

Virginia saw her daughter stiffen from the corner of her eye. She said, "This place meant everything to Dad."

Ephraim pointed at the window. "Your father gave his life to that ground and burning sun out there. He walked away from a full professorship and offered his soul to both of them, and they both accepted it without mercy or appreciation."

"He was happy."

Ephraim shook his head. "You didn't see the change in him when you came back"—he motioned at Piper and Bran —"with those young ones in tow. *That* was his happiness, Virginia. *That* became his life. You didn't know him before that. You didn't see what the land was doing to him. He came back from the dead when he saw you at the gate."

Virginia said nothing.

"Besides, you can't keep this place up—you and Cotton. Look at how it's already getting away from you."

"We'll let the bottomlands go," Virginia said. "We don't need its production anyway." She paused. "I like it here."

Ephraim leaned forward. "Are you waiting for someone to arrive at the gate too?"

Virginia didn't answer.

Ephraim said, "Take Luke with you."

She looked at him.

"I've had my life," he said, "but yours"—he gestured at the children again—"and *theirs* are just beginning. Leave, Virginia. When you make a child you also make a promise. You're a parent, and parents don't get the luxury of choice."

"You couldn't survive without Luke."

Ephraim shrugged.

"Don't you dare, Ephraim. Don't you dare talk like that."

"We all wet our tongues with the nectar of our choices," Ephraim said. "Like everyone's, mine's been sweet and bitter, and I've not the time left for different decisions or new directions. The sand falls quickly through the hour-glass, Virginia, and blessed are those wise enough to use up all the grains allotted them."

Virginia shook her head.

"Make an old man happy and tell me you'll go."

"I won't leave you."

He stood and cupped her face in his hands again, gently ran his thumb over the scar on her forehead. "We all leave someday, my girl. And you wouldn't be abandoning me;

you'd be ensuring our young ones have a life, the opportunity to make choices of their own. You'd be giving them that which I can't. And you'd allow me the chance to look back from that yonder shore and know I did my best."

Virginia said nothing.

"Will you give them your best too?" Ephraim asked. "For me?"

Virginia's eyes welled.

VIRGINIA STOOD in a valley between two mountains, a cool river swirling around her ankles and a breeze washing over her face and neck.

The sun was deep in its descent, leaving one slope bathed in yellow light while the other was slowly clothed in shadow.

And though she loathed the thought of leaving the water, she felt drawn toward one of the mountains, an inexplicable pull that seemed from without as well as within. But she wasn't sure from which peak it beckoned.

And then she heard a call, someone repeating a name that was hers and not hers. But like the mysterious draw from the mountain, she couldn't determine the direction of the voice. It seemed close, all around her, *from* her, but—

She jerked up and threw out her hand.

Bran let go of her arm and stumbled back.

Virginia took a breath, blew it out. She glanced at the dark windows as she settled back in her chair.

Bran said, "Why are you sleeping at the table, Mama?"

"I was just ..."—she paused—"thinking."

"Didn't you sleep at the table last night too?" Bran asked.

"Little bit, I guess."

Virginia leaned back. Her back was stiff and sore and tied in knots. She felt like she'd been thrown from a horse, or kicked by one. "Why are you still awake?" she asked.

"I was wondering if you'd tuck us in like you used to? Maybe tell us a story?"

Virginia ran a hand through her son's hair, let her fingers linger on his cheek. "I doubt Piper'd be interested in such things anymore."

"Just me, then."

The anticipation and longing in Bran's soft features took her off guard. Though outwardly growing like a weed, he was still so young and innocent, so oblivious to the world outside. She saw Landry in his big hopeful eyes. She saw her father too.

"Don't reckon I know any fresh stories," she said. "You've already heard all the old tales."

"We'll make it work."

Virginia smiled at that. "All right, little man."

PIPER SLAMMED the drawer in her end table when Virginia and Bran entered the room. She spun around and said, "*What*?"

Virginia eyed the drawer, then Piper.

Piper leaned back against the old wooden dresser.

Virginia pointed at her daughter's bed and Piper moved away and sat by her pillow, grabbing Virginia's arm as she did.

"What are you doing in here?" Piper asked.

Bran piled onto his bed and bounced up and down on the blanket. "She's going to tell us a story."

Virginia looked at Piper's hand and Piper let go.

"Oh," Piper said.

Virginia finished dragging her chair inside their bedroom. When she sat down, her lower back sent a lightning bolt of pain all the way into her neck. She leaned forward and placed her head in her hands.

"You okay, Mama?" Piper asked.

"Trying to think of a story."

"Tell us about when Grandpa outfoxed Crazy Horse," Bran said.

Piper moaned. "No, think of something else."

"Come on," Bran pleaded.

"You already know that one back and through," Virginia said.

Bran slid to the edge of his bed. "I'll tell it then. One day when Grandpa was out hunting, he came across Crazy Horse—"

"No, Bran," Piper said. "Grandpa wasn't hunting."

"It's when he was traveling here from back east," Virginia said.

"That part don't matter no way," Bran said. "Anyhow, when he met up with Crazy Horse, Crazy Horse shot at him and Grandpa dodged the bullet."

"No, Bran." Piper was shaking her head.

"*Uh-huh.*"

"He pointed at him, son," Virginia said. "Your grandpa was on one ridge and Crazy Horse was on another. Your grandpa said they watched each other for a minute or two then Crazy Horse raised a finger and pointed at him."

"Didn't Crazy Horse have a pistol in his hand?"

"No, honey. You have to remember things right."

Bran frowned. "Still must've been scary, though."

"Truly."

"'Cause Crazy Horse would've killed and scalped him, right?"

Virginia thought about it. "It's not always easy to know what folks will or won't do."

"But that's what Indians do, right?"

"Not all of them, son. You remember Horseshoe Jim, don't you?"

"Uh-huh."

"You remember how nice he was to you?"

Bran nodded but seemed unconvinced.

"How'd he know it was Crazy Horse?" Piper asked. "Grandpa, I mean?"

Virginia leaned back in her chair. "I don't know. I guess I never asked him."

Bran said, "It was definitely Crazy Horse! Y'all ain't changing that part!"

Virginia laughed.

Piper pointed at her brother. "You said '*ain't*'!"

Bran laughed, too, though reluctantly. Then he frowned and looked at Virginia. "Mama, who keeps looking in the window behind you?"

Virginia whirled and aimed her shotgun at the window. The glass was dark and empty, only the slightest glaze of moonlight reflecting on its surface.

She kicked her chair aside and began backing away. "Get to the loft."

"Where'd you have that scattergun?" Piper asked.

Virginia tucked the weapon back under her coat. "The loft, Piper."

"Mama, what's—"

"Now!"

LIKE THE WINDOW in Piper and Bran's bedroom, the front porch was also dark and quiet.

Virginia left the door ajar and eased down the front of the house to avoid being backlit by the lantern inside. She wondered if she should call out to Cotton. She wondered if Bran's imagination had gotten the better of him.

That's when her feet tangled in the burlap sack on the porch. She picked it up. The material had three holes in it, two where the eyes should be and one ragged tear in the forehead.

"*Peekaboo ...*"

Virginia dropped below the hand railing and looked north where the voice had come from.

"*I seee you ...*"

Virginia turned. Another voice from the south. A second man. One of them on each flank.

She shrugged out of her coat and slipped the shotgun's strap off her shoulder.

Then another voice from the dark front yard: "*Where's the baby?*"

And still another, from what sounded like directly above her: "*There's the baby!*"

Virginia backpedaled, slipped and fell. She dropped to a knee and leaned against a support beam.

Laughter.

"Yes, that was a sweet scene if I ever did see one—you and them young'uns. Come now and send that pretty little girl out here. They say delay is the worst part, you know. Think it through, lady. You're all alone out here, and we can take this place any time we like. You do understand that, don't you?"

Virginia did understand. She understood that she was naked from her position on the porch. She'd made herself vulnerable by walking straight out the door like an idiot. *Stupid*.

She said, "What do you want?"

Another voice. This man dead ahead. "We know what you're planning, Ms. Cooper. Big open country. Probably figure it's easy to move around in, easy to sneak off. Bet that old man thought so too. But hear me, woman: their ain't no deliverance out there, ain't no way to outrun the stars in the sky."

Virginia glanced around the column, toward the direction of the voice.

A shot splintered the wood above her head and she ducked.

More laughter.

"What was his name—that old man? Why do you reckon he was so reluctant to tell us? And where do you suppose his boy went?"

Virginia's spine turned cold; a hundred icy needles swam through her guts. She stood, switched the shotgun to her left hand, and reached around the small of her back. She screamed, "Ephraim!"

"Oh, no. He's not with us anymore, darlin'. But he was a tough old bird, a friend to you 'til the last. He even took a shot at us, the old bastard, killed his own horse in the process. But he yielded, little lady, same as you will in the end."

The man in front of the house stepped into the light from the window, the one the others had called Cyrus. He was close now, but still clear from the effective range of the shotgun.

Virginia took a step toward him and two more men emerged from the north and south.

Cyrus raised a hand of invitation. "Got your lather up, huh? Come on and let us get this over with then."

Virginia gripped her shotgun. Three in view now, all in front of her. At least two more hidden in the night.

"*Mama*?" Bran's voice from inside the house.

Cyrus said, "Last chance to avoid needless suffering. If you force our hand, we'll gladly consider other measures. And we're good at such things, Ms. Cooper. Like the rattler in high grass, or the spider dropping from the ceiling, you'll not find a place where we're not already there. That's your world now."

Virginia backed into the house, her eyes never leaving Cyrus's. She closed and bolted the door and then slumped against the wall.

The frame of the house shivered beneath the movements of the one on the roof. She heard a horse snort, muffled voices, then the porch creaking.

The door quivered against the iron bolt, rattled, jerked, and then nothing.

Silence.

Virginia pounded the wall, her knees and legs. She gripped her hair, spoke Ephraim's name over and over.

And when she looked up and saw the expressions on her children's faces, she turned away and sobbed.

8

_____

Hux rolled over, pushed himself to his feet and looked out the window. He had no idea how long he'd been sleeping on the floor at the front of the tavern, just that it wasn't long enough.

He'd spent all night, the entire morning, and some of the afternoon searching for Brady's killer. And both he and every other member of the group had come up empty.

They'd found the guy's tracks well enough, and presumably Sally White Horse's, both retreating through the dirt around the dry-goods store and into the countryside. But that was all. No other traces.

Elias Haynes, the group's finest scout and tracker, and one of its oldest members, had gone out at daybreak. But he'd also returned with nothing to report.

Hux sat across from Zalen.

Zalen gestured at Gavin and Amos, who were leaning against the bar. "Cyrus has relayed some intriguing information to us."

Gavin and Amos had returned from the south last

night. But Cyrus, Quinn, and Otto were still out there doing God only knew what.

Hux said, "We could've used him and those other four men last night."

Zalen gave him a look and Hux held his tongue.

Zalen said, "You have seen a jigsaw puzzle, correct?"

Hux nodded.

"Then I assume you've noticed that even while the puzzle is incomplete, while it still has missing pieces, the image is already taking shape."

"Yeah."

"Well," Zalen said, "I have discovered life to be that way as well. If one is patient, if one waits for the next piece to present itself, then—"

The front door swung open and Ashe entered, pushing Everett Reeves ahead of him.

Zalen sat back. "Ah, the good sheriff. And just in time."

Ashe shoved the sheriff close to Zalen's table.

"Have you any news of my missing property?" Zalen asked.

The sheriff stared at his hands, shook his head.

"Yes," Zalen said. "Why am I not surprised." He looked at Hux. "Please be sure to update the good sheriff's wife on his progress."

Hux nodded.

Zalen said, "Now, dear Sheriff, about this man we seek. I wish for you to tell me about him."

The sheriff looked at Hux and Ashe. "I don't know him. I swear it on my mother's grave."

"You have seen him then?" Zalen asked.

"I've never put eyes on the man."

"Then how is it you can be so certain you don't know him?"

The sheriff took a breath, wrung his hands. "I ... There ain't no one around here who'd—"

Zalen held up a hand. "Do not be anxious, Sheriff. You are in no danger here. As it turns out, I believe you. I think you would be more than eager to assist us if you could, given what you have at stake. But that is neither here nor there. That is not why we required your presence today."

Zalen looked at Hux. "I believe retrieving Mrs. Odom to be our most pressing matter at present."

Hux looked a question at him.

Zalen said, "I assume you noticed how the young widow protected her womb during our visit?"

Hux nodded. He had noticed. He'd seen her hand go to her stomach when Zalen struck her the second time.

"Think of it this way, Mr. Huxtable. We accomplish two things by placing Mrs. Odom against the wall. First, we keep our promise—two for one. We also deny this town hope, which is infinitely more important than you've yet learned. Second, we protect ourselves from future retribution."

Hux looked dubious.

"Consider this," Zalen said, "by eliminating Mrs. Odom and her unborn, we remove the possibility of a vengeful son or daughter arriving at our door in the future. We guarantee that, whatever our end, it will not be at the hands of this dead lawman's child. We take that potentiality away forever."

Hux said, "What about the guy we've been—"

"Mr. Ashner will take care of our insurgent," Zalen

said.

The sheriff spoke up, though there was a noticeable tremble in his voice. "Julie's no threat to you. She's one woman, lost and alone. Hell, without Donovan she'll need help just to get by." He stopped, though it was clear he wanted to say more.

Zalen said, "I am aware of her gender, dear Sheriff. And really, you should be pleased at this. We'll be doing your township a favor, pruning the herd, as it were. You and your people will be free to focus your concerns elsewhere."

"She won't come with you," the sheriff said. "She'll—"

"I have considered she is probably desperate," Zalen interrupted. "And, of course, I understand she may not easily submit. She might even stand and resist, attempt to preserve herself. I am sometimes surprised by women.

"That is why I'm sending you to retrieve her, Sheriff. Even given your failure to protect her husband, I believe she will trust you. She will listen to you, see you as a confidant and ally. And your actions, however unpleasant they may be, will cost you nothing more than your soul, which, in my opinion, will only make you a better lawman in the future."

The sheriff looked away.

Zalen leaned forward. "And though I can only suppose this is the case, I imagine any good husband thinks first and foremost of his beloved, even when it makes him uncomfortable. Would that be right, Everett?"

The sheriff grimaced, nodded.

PIPER FOLLOWED her mother into the daylight of the front yard. Her mom looked at the ridge to the north for a long time, then to the forest and river to the west, before finally turning her attention to Cotton.

Cotton said, "Yes'um."

Her mom sat down on the porch and started rolling a cigarette, something Piper had only seen her do a few times.

"Mama?"

To Cotton, her mom said, "They'll be back. We've got to lock it down; I mean everything. Maybe board the windows, double bolt the doors. We have to make it hard on them."

Cotton said nothing.

"And you're gonna have to come inside, Cotton," her mom said. "You can't be out here alone when they show again."

Cotton lowered his head.

Piper glanced at the house.

BRAN HAD CRIED and Piper had questioned long into the night, and both had been met with mostly silence. Her mom had kept telling them to sleep, that they were going to need all their rest now, which Piper had thought impossible.

But as her mom rocked Bran and hummed and stroked Piper's hair, sleep had eventually come. And when Piper had woken in the loft, her mom was sitting in the same place by the door again, her back against the wall, her head slumped against her knees.

PIPER SAID, "Mama, where's Luke? He's okay, isn't he?"

Her mom went on grappling with the cigarette, biting her lower lip.

She finally handed the paper and tobacco to Cotton, who finished rolling them for her—which seemed a wonder to Piper, considering the size of the big man's fingers.

"Mama, I'm worried about—"

"I know, Piper."

"But ..."

Her mom lit the smoke, got up and moved aimlessly into the yard, her eyes never leaving the ridge or horizon beyond the front gate, the cigarette burning away between her fingers.

Piper walked toward the barn. She thought about what Luke had said the day before, wondered which direction he'd gone. He'd said he would be back as quick as he could, and that's what she'd wanted to hear at the time. But now ... now she just wanted him to stay away, stay away as long as possible. But even more than that, she wanted to find him, warn him, tell him about his father. She had to, had to figure out a way.

When she looked back, her mom was glaring at her. The expression on her face was a familiar one, the *don't you dare* look Piper had seen hundreds of times. But it was also sharp and cold and had a quality Piper didn't recognize. It looked like someone else was staring at her. It made her skin cool and tingly.

Her mom said, "*In the house.*"

EVERETT HAD BANGED on both doors and every window he could reach. He'd peered through each opening he could find, every crack, uneven joint and board. Finally, he'd kicked the door in and gone inside.

The place was empty, not empty as in cleaned out or packed up and abandoned, but lifeless. Julie wasn't there.

Everett immediately thought the worst, that the trauma and stress of losing Donovan had pushed her into the unthinkable. He'd seen it before.

He tore through the house and then ran outside, searching the surrounding woodlands and calling her name, all the while assuring her in his calmest voice that everything was okay, all the while fearing the fires of hell for doing so.

But there was no response. She was nowhere to be found.

Everett finally gave up his search inside the barn and slumped against an empty stall. That's when he noticed the two bare hooks on the opposite wall. He remembered Donovan hanging his saddle on one of them. And though he hadn't been out here since they'd been married, the other hook, he knew, had been installed for Julie. It was new and brass and shiny, and exactly like something Donovan would've done for his beloved bride.

Donovan.

Everett frowned. Like the house, the barn was also devoid of life, no horses, mules, or anything else stirring. Julie was gone and he was alone.

Until the shadow passed along the wall from the outside, moving past one sunlit gap in the framing to the next, like a silent heartbeat or ticking clock.

Everett instinctively reached for his revolver before remembering Zalen's men had taken it from him.

He said, "Hey! You there!"

A pause.

"*Hold*." Everett enunciated the word with all the authority he could muster, then started toward the door.

The shadow began moving again.

Everett stopped, knowing he couldn't make it outside in time to stop the guy if he bolted. He returned to the wall.

"I said *hold*! This is Sheriff Reeves. Identify yourself."

The man kept moving.

"Wait! Please. I mean you no harm. I've just got to find Julie. She's the woman of this place. Julie Odom. Just tell me if you've seen her?"

No answer.

"Look, mister, this is important. She needs to come with me right now."

Silence.

"Listen, I know what you're thinking, but it's me, Everett Reeves. You know you can talk to me. I'm not one of them."

"Then why are you here?"

"Jesus, are you deaf?" Everett said. "I need to find Julie. She has to come into town with me. It's urgent."

"Why?"

"Because I said so! Do you know who I am?"

"You're a coward."

Everett slapped the wall. "You don't know a damn thing about me, mister. So don't you go—"

"I know what they did to your deputies."

Everett said nothing.

"And I know what they're doing to your town."

"Yeah, and what am I supposed to do?" Everett said. "I

can't take down some twenty men alone. Should I just die with the rest of them?"

"Yes."

"Easy for you to judge," Everett said, "creeping around in the shadows, hiding behind walls. Why don't you come in here and—"

"I'm looking for Mason."

Everett's breath caught. He placed a hand on the wall. "Lord in heaven, you're the one they're searching for. You're the one who stirred this whole thing up. You've got to come with me. You *will* come with me. I'm taking you back."

"You're not able to take me back."

"Damn you to hell!" Everett slapped the wall again, dug his fingers into the wood. "Look, I'll do anything, whatever you ask, but you have to come with me."

"I'm looking for Mason."

"I don't know any Masons," Everett said. Then: "*Wait* ..." He thought hard, searched his memory, fell just short of banging his head against the inside of the barn. "The only Mason I knew died in the war."

The man started moving again.

"Stop, mister. We're not done. I'm bringing you in if it kills me."

"It will."

Everett pressed himself against the wall. "This isn't me!" he shouted. "I swear it. They've got my wife. They've taken my Theresa. Don't you understand? They've already maimed her because of me and promised more if I don't do their bidding."

"Where is she?"

"I don't know. For God's sake, you think I'd be *here* if I knew?" Everett lowered his head and wrung his hands. "You can end this, mister. Don't you get it? They're going to find you anyway. So just come with me now and they'll stop the killing. They might even let you walk, you know, out of respect. Just think about the lives you'll be saving. If it's not Julie, it'll be someone else."

Everett looked up, hopeful his blend of truth and lies had sounded more persuasive in the stranger's ears than his own.

But the man was gone.

OTTO CLINE STUMBLED through the door of the tavern.

Hux spun around and Ashe raised his rifle.

Otto leaned against the wall. He said, "Oh God, Zee. Is Cyrus and Quinn here?"

Zalen didn't look at him. "Am I Mr. Kane's keeper?"

"No, no, I just mean has anyone seen them?"

"I am sure they'll be along," Zalen said.

Otto looked at the floor, looked at his hands. He finally walked behind the bar, uncorked a bottle and took a long swallow. He paused as the burn washed through him, then placed his hand on the counter. "I saw him, Zee. I saw the son of a bitch that killed Chester."

"And you waited more than twelve hours to report?"

"I was looking for Cyrus and Quinn. We were supposed to ... Oh God, Zee, the screaming." Otto closed his eyes and took another drink. "Cyrus wanted to take that ranch on the other side of the river. He wanted them to think we were gone. So we crossed the bridge and split up, planning to recross the river at different places and meet at the rear of the property.

"I waited," Otto went on, "but Cyrus and Quinn, they never showed. Then I heard the wailing. It was awful, Zee." He rubbed his arms. "Like animals being slaughtered. But it wasn't animals. It was them. I know it was them."

"And you saw our mystery man?"

"Yeah, right after I found Cyrus and Quinn's horses. They'd never even recrossed the river. That's when I saw the bastard. He was right there in the woods near the bridge, standing in the trees like the night itself."

"And you didn't pursue him?"

"I did, Zee. I shot at him. I fired and fired until my rifle was empty. But he was just gone, man. No blood, no tracks, no horse. I looked for him all night, for Cyrus and Quinn, too, but—"

"It is *el Coco*."

The soft feminine voice caught them all off guard.

Hux turned as Moriya soundlessly crossed the room behind them.

She said, "*El Coco's* time has come, and he has chosen the form that pleases him. Just like in the days of old, he comes now to punish the wicked and take away the disobedient."

Zalen grinned, incredulous. "Whatever shall we do then, Ms. Moriya? Shall we flee to the mountains? Shall we call on the gods to deliver us from the boogeyman? Should we hunker down, lock and bolt the doors?"

Moriya placed her hand on the door. "I will kill *el Coco* because I do not fear him. But not before he takes more of you, perhaps many more. This is his dark sacred night."

9

Hux stared at the bodies of Cyrus and Quinn—the stabs, cuts, and mutilations, the cold water draining color from their skin.

Hux had been in the military, had risen in rank during a period when it was not easy to do so. He'd seen action in the Indian Wars, learned tactics, maneuvers, and protocols —all reasons Zalen kept him close, he knew.

He'd also left the military as soon as he could, actually sooner. He abandoned the blue uniform after the Battle of the Big Hole, slipping away after the fight and assumed dead. Nonetheless, he'd been around long enough to see the worst side of humanity. He'd seen men tortured, heard women and children wailing and begging to empty gray skies. He'd seen all of them dead at some point—all ages, races, and backgrounds.

And though he'd heard such things described by an occasional drunk or battle-weary soldier, he'd never seen anything like this firsthand.

Elias Haynes gestured at the bodies. "The man who did this has blood as cold as that water."

Hux didn't disagree. Cyrus and Quinn had been gutted, opened up from groin to gullet. He'd seen animals in this state, but never a man.

They'd yet to locate Cyrus's pistol, but Quinn's revolver had still been holstered at his side, and both men's rifles were secured in scabbards on their horses. None of the weapons had been fired.

Hux looked around. "Where are the tracks?"

"Not any."

"How could there be no tracks?"

"They weren't put in the water here." Elias looked upriver. "They never recrossed; you can tell that from the horses' tracks. Unless they did it on foot, which means they were bigger fools than I thought."

Elias thought about it. "No, they were killed upstream and the current towed them into this snag of brush."

"Can you find them?" Hux asked. "The tracks, I mean?"

"If I gave it enough time. But what good would it do now?"

Hux said nothing.

"I've seen this before," Elias said, which surprised Hux, but the old scout didn't elaborate.

"What was Moriya talking about back there?" Hux asked. "Who was she—"

"*El Coco*," Elias said. "The Mexican boogeyman. Comes in the night to take away evildoers or some such. Some say he's the night itself, that the darkness sometimes comes to life to claim the souls of the lost."

"You believe such things?"

Elias shrugged. "Who knows? But if there is such an avenging angel, it ain't no surprise he'd strike this bunch."

Hux was again taken aback by the comment. He said, "Why do you do this?"

"What else would I do? Farm? I'm already going to hell for what I did during the war. Might as well not starve on the way."

Hux looked at the scout, who'd turned his gaze downriver.

Elias said, "Don't ever ask me that again."

"Okay."

"And don't ask anyone else either, lest you want Zalen to put you against the wall."

THEY BURIED Cyrus and Quinn just inside the tree line near the river. As darkness fell, Hux and Elias settled down on the riverbank while the other members of the group— some eight or ten of them—remained concealed in the woods on either flank.

The hope was that their guy would see the two of them sitting alone, apparently isolated and vulnerable, and present himself, same as he'd probably done with Cyrus and Quinn. Easy pickings. And then the hidden members of the group would emerge from the forest and close the net around him.

It was a standard trick, probably as old as time itself, but it worked. Hux had even seen the trap successfully deployed against the Indians, who sometimes seemed to possess an almost mystical ability to sniff out an ambush.

Even so, Hux knew it was a long shot. Zalen had instructed him to locate their missing men, but also to bring back the insurgent, in any way or state he saw fit. It was the best idea he could come up with.

So they waited, and waited. And nothing happened.

After an hour or so Hux saw one of the group members roaming in the moonlight near the river. The man moved along the northern banks of the water for a minute or two and then disappeared back into the forest.

Hux shook his head and looked at Elias, who'd also noticed the wanderer.

"They're getting restless," Elias said.

"They're not taking this serious."

"Don't matter anyhow. Our man's too smart for such an obvious snare."

"I've seen far better men go for it," Hux said. "And this guy's shown nothing but cowardice so far."

Elias spat. "A man who yields for no good reason is a coward. The fella who dives headlong into an untenable position is a fool. There's plenty of both—some are among us tonight—and most are not long for this world." The scout shook his head. "The man we're after is neither."

"You respect him after what he did to Cyrus and Quinn?"

"If you don't respect him," Elias said, "you'll *be* Cyrus and Quinn."

Hux said nothing. He watched as the wanderer returned—a silhouette some two hundred yards away—moving farther north up the riverbank and then disappearing again back into the forest.

Hux stood and brushed himself off. "This is pointless."

He motioned to the north. "They might as well build a brush fire. The way they're moving about, everybody in the—"

Two quick gunshots, right together, a sharp split in the dark silence.

Hux looked at Elias.

Elias narrowed his eyes.

Hux said, "Damned if it didn't work after all."

Elias grinned at the surprise in Hux's voice. The scout was obviously surprised too.

That's when the godawful screaming began. That terrible, soul-shearing wailing Otto Cline had described.

GAVIN SAID, "MY ASS IS NUMB."

Amos grunted. "That damn knot on your shoulders is too."

Gavin turned and looked at Amos, but Amos kept searching the forest.

"What I mean is this is stupid," Gavin said. "Why would we just sit here and wait for him? Didn't you see their bodies?"

"Damn right I saw 'em. And I'm going to gut that bastard, same as he did Cyrus and Quinn. 'Cept I'm gonna take my time, nice and slow. And I ain't gonna let him down 'till he's empty of tears."

Gavin said nothing.

"And, Gavin."

"Yeah?"

"If you get up and commence to wandering again, I'll be starting with you."

Gavin's mouth opened and closed. He eventually looked away, but Amos could tell he was itching to say something.

Amos resumed studying the forest. His range of sight was mere feet now in the darkness. But like any good predator, he knew a successful hunt didn't involve only the eyes but the full spectrum of one's senses. And he *was* a predator, had been since he first stood and started walking.

Sounds came and went in the woods—the swish of leaves, the snap of sticks and twigs, the occasional chirp or grunt of an animal. All natural occurrences, all day, all night.

Such things disturbed lesser men. Amos had seen would-be hunters wet their britches over the simplest noises in the forest. Still others might rise and begin blind-firing their weapons into the trees and brush.

Half-wits, all of them. Most failed to understand the quiet nudges of the real hunter, the internal pull in one direction instead of another, the instincts of a true killer.

Amos had considered that he alone possessed such powers, that either no one else had them or no one else recognized them. But that was neither here nor there at the moment. Because Amos was feeling them now, his body alive and tingling with the sensations—the prickle of hair on his arms, the cooling in his blood, the inexorable pull toward the north.

He nudged Gavin and nodded over his shoulder. "Go tell Karl and Hank to move up."

"And leave you?"

"How the hell else you gonna do it?" Amos said. "And

don't you make a sound. If I so much as hear you breathe, you better hope you never see me again."

Gavin said, "How am I gonna find 'em if I can't make noise? They'll shoot me in this dark."

Amos withdrew his revolver and eased the hammer back.

Gavin got up and moved away, searching the ground for loose sticks or leaves before each step.

Amos turned back to the forest, back to his instincts, back to that infallible part of himself that had kept him alive all these years, kept him unbeaten. Undefeated.

He spoke through clenched teeth. "Let's dance, you son of a bitch."

The blade's first bite was cold in his back, a shard of ice wedged against his lower rib, in and out and gone.

Amos whirled and loosed two quick shots, working the hammer as fast as he could.

The blade's second thrust caught him in the abdomen and then jerked up. And this time it was hot iron, a long smoldering ember tearing and twisting in his gut. The pain was blinding, like nothing Amos could've imagined or described.

He heard himself screaming, felt his back slap against the ground. His hands and arms flailed and searched for his fallen pistol, but there was only the pain now, only the white-hot fire devouring his insides and mind.

He felt shame and fear, and then, when he heard Gavin's panicked voice calling his name, sympathy.

. . .

It took Hux twenty full minutes to catch up to Elias, who'd seemingly disappeared once they entered the woods to the north. When he did catch up, the old scout was already walking the ground around the bodies.

Elias knelt and pointed at something in the leaves. "I figure Gavin circled back when he heard the screaming, and our guy put him down here from behind. Looks like he crawled the rest of the way."

"You find the bastard's tracks?" Hux asked.

Elias squinted at the ground. "They're all over. I suspect we're standing on most of 'em."

Amos and Gavin hadn't been mutilated like the previous two, but the results were the same. Their end had also come at the edge of a blade, but the knife work had been more efficient this time, lacking the malice visited on Cyrus and Quinn.

"Can we give chase?" Hux asked.

Elias shook his head. "Not in this environment, and definitely not in the dark. We'd have to spread out again."

"There's still nine of us," Hux said, incredulous.

"He picked his spot," Elias said. "He knew what we were doing and chose to hit our flank." The scout looked at Hux. "We're in his web and he's taking us apart one piece at a time."

Another shot went off, the third time a nervous trigger finger had gotten the better of the remaining men since the attacks.

"Hold your fire!" Hux shouted.

The group had formed a semicircle around the bodies, and they were edgy, all of them. Hux had heard the name *el Coco* whispered more than once. He'd also heard his own name a couple of times, prefixed with terms of derision that he himself had hurled at incompetent officers back when he wore the uniform.

"What then?" Hux said. "You suggesting we pull back?"

"Yes."

"He's one man."

"Sometimes it's better to be alone."

Hux wasn't sure how to take that.

"He's got the advantage in these woods," Elias said. "You're worried about Zalen when you should be worried about these men."

Hux shook his head. "He could be right here, Elias." He waved a hand at the woods. "Right out there."

Elias said nothing.

Hux blew out a breath. "Pull back to where?"

"Town."

"We have to bury these two first."

"Not now."

"Dammit, Elias, we have to. We can't leave them like this."

The old scout studied Hux a beat. Then: "All right."

Hux slumped to the floor in the front of the tavern when they returned, the same place where he'd been sleeping the last few days.

Elias shook him hours later, but Hux was already awake, just lying there staring at the wall. He'd woken to the screaming and gunshots an hour before, the crying and pleading and begging that seemed to go on and on without end, until it didn't.

Zalen had killed three townspeople that morning. He'd wanted to put eight against the wall, but Ashe could only locate three more, all of whom the assassin killed himself during the roundup—those who'd made the mistake of resisting him.

Hux said, "He's losing it, isn't he? Zalen's losing it."

Elias grunted. "This is who Zalen is. You just haven't been around long enough. He keeps his promises."

Hux said nothing.

"He's instructed us to retrieve the sheriff's wife," Elias said, "said he's got no use for either of them anymore. And the two of them make eight."

Hux closed his eyes.

"Right now," Elias said.

THE RIDE to the abandoned barn took half an hour. Hux had chosen the place because the inside had been stripped bare, either by the original owners or scavengers later on. He'd initially thought it strange to find such a pristine building deserted. But then, considering the circumstances in this town, what else would one expect?

He'd left two chairs facing each other in the center of the place—one for the guard he'd posted to keep an eye on Theresa Reeves, the other for the sheriff's wife herself.

Both seats were empty.

Hux ran a hand over his face.

Elias searched the inside, no doubt trying to interpret any evidence the floor might offer. He studied the ground around the vacant chairs for a long time and then eventually slipped through the side door into the sunlight outside.

Hux moved to the center of the room and sat where the sheriff's wife should've been. The ropes that had bound her in the seat were piled in heaps at the chair's legs.

Hux put his head in his hands.

He tried to remember how long it had been since he'd been out here. A day, a day and a half? Probably more like two. Adrenaline and lack of sleep had loosened his grip on the passage of time. He wondered how far Theresa Reeves could've gotten on foot, and if there was any chance of pursuing her. And if he wanted to pursue her. He also wondered if Zalen had ever put a member of the group against the wall.

He heard Elias come back in and sit down in the chair across from him.

Hux didn't bother raising his head. "Any luck?" he asked, though he found he didn't really care what the scout had to say.

When Elias didn't answer, Hux leaned back and rubbed his eyes, which were dry and felt full of dirt. Then he let out a breath, shook his head, and said, "Shit."

Because the man sitting opposite him wasn't Elias.

10

Bran moved his checker piece in front of Piper's, giddy with anticipation of his next move, literally vibrating. But then Piper jumped his piece and took it off the board, same as she had the last one he left vulnerable, over and over, time after time. Bran just wouldn't learn.

Cotton watched from the chair under the window where her mom had instructed him to stay. Before that he would sit, stand, look out the window, and then pace the front of the house, all inside of a minute's time, all like clockwork.

It wasn't until her mom said, "Please sit down, Cotton," that he finally planted himself in the chair and removed his knife and hunk of wood.

He pretended to be whittling or carving or whatever he did, but Piper knew he was watching them. She'd caught him staring twice, which made her skin itchy. So she finally turned her back to him, effectively blocking his view.

Bran was oblivious. He was too busy contemplating which of his next pieces to sacrifice.

. . .

PIPER FINISHED off Bran and walked out onto the front porch where her mom was sitting. She noticed Cotton tense and his eyes widen as she got up, but she ignored him.

Once the door was closed behind her, Piper said, "Can't you tell him to go outside?"

Her mom was reclining in her rocker, staring at the same map she'd been poring over all day—details of the surrounding area and countryside that Piper hadn't even known existed, never mind seen for herself.

The map had been sketched on a soft material Piper didn't recognize. It looked like some sort of fabric, only thicker and coarse. Piper had never seen such a thing, nor at this particular moment did she care about its qualities or uniqueness. She was only concerned over what it represented.

Her mom was tracing the hand-drawn lines with the tips of her fingers and seemed to be in a place a great distance away from the front porch.

Piper waited for an answer that didn't come. Finally, she said, "Did Ephraim draw that?"

A nod.

"Are we going somewhere?"

Her mom didn't answer.

Piper ground her teeth, bit her lip, then hopped in place and snatched the map from her mom's hand. "No! We're not leaving without Luke!" She'd barely finished the sentence before her whole body tensed in anticipation of her mom's backlash.

But even as her mom turned and looked at her, Piper

forged ahead. "We're not even looking for him, Mama. And you're just sitting here like nothing's wrong, like you don't care. And when you're not in this chair, you're—" She waved a hand toward the land out front. "And you won't let us out of the house, and you won't make Cotton go away, and ..."

Piper stopped and rubbed her arms.

Her mom watched her, eyes probing in that uncomfortable way only hers could. But there was a softness, too, a hint of grief or pain so foreign on her it actually scared Piper, and hurt her soul.

"I'm sorry, Mama. It's just ..."

Her mom reached up and placed a hand on Piper's cheek. "I won't leave him, baby girl. I won't ever leave any of you."

Piper held up the map. "Then why do you keep looking at this?"

"Do you believe me?" her mom asked.

Piper swallowed.

"Do you believe me, baby?"

Piper nodded.

"Do you know how I love you?"

"Yes, ma'am."

Her mom looked down, like the answer had somehow missed the mark. She said, "Tell me everything Luke said to you."

Piper did, for the third time. Not everything, of course. She left out the part about Luke's future wife.

Her mom's attention drifted away again, and Piper hoped she was thinking the same as her. *An errand*? Why would Ephraim send him out now? And alone? It infuriated her. It didn't make sense. Nothing made sense anymore. She hoped her mom saw that too.

Piper was tired of it all, tired of waiting, and worrying, and praying, and Cotton, and ... *everything*. It was time to tell her mom, confess that she and Luke were going to be married. Her mom needed to know how important he was to her. She needed to take this seriously.

But just as she mounted her courage, her mom suddenly stood and looked west. The thin lines at her eyes tightened and deepened. Her lips pursed the way they did when she was puzzled or worrying over something. But there was also that faraway look again. The same one Piper knew signaled her to keep her mouth shut.

THE MAN WAS TURNING a coin between his thumb and first two fingers, while the middle finger of his other hand tapped the handle of the knife sheathed at his hip. A revolver was holstered cross-draw on his opposite side, the way Hux had seen some card players carry their weapons.

Hux felt the weight of his own pistol tugging at his belt, but there was no way he could draw it fast enough given his position on the chair. He glanced at the side door of the barn.

The man said, "Your friend won't be joining us."

"What did you do to him?" Hux asked. "Elias wasn't ..." *Wasn't what*? What was Hux going to say? *Elias wasn't a threat to you. Elias wasn't like the rest.* Neither of which could be claimed with a straight face.

The stranger watched him, still turning the tarnished silver coin, still tapping the handle of that terrible blade.

Hux was struck by the simplicity of the man, the unremarkable features and build. He was thin and pale and had a weariness behind his eyes Hux recognized. He was any man on the street, or farm—except he wasn't.

"You can't win this," Hux said. "Whatever you do to me, there'll be more of them coming, and more after that. They'll never let up. They're not allowed to.

"And by resisting," Hux went on, "you're only killing more innocents. Haven't you heard what Zalen did today? He's repaying your actions to the townspeople. And he's just getting started. That's on your soul, too, mister. His and your sins are entwined now."

"Like killing women?"

"Women?" Hux said. "You mean Tess? How do you know about that?"

"People talk."

"Who? Cyrus?" Hux asked, voice rising. "Did you torture it out of him? Did he tell you that before you castrated him and cut him open like a game deer?"

"Did he deserve it?"

"Of course he deserved it," Hux said. "But who could do such a thing? You're not human. You're worse than Zalen."

The man said nothing.

"And you didn't know Tess. She was one of them. Hell, given the chance, she would've killed the lot of us herself."

The man grinned.

"You don't understand, mister," Hux said. "The women in this group, they're killers, all of them. Zalen prefers it that way. He wants women because he says no one expects them, and he's right. He says it's hard to find a tough woman; otherwise, I think the whole group would be female."

"Tough women are everywhere," the man said. "It's hard to find an evil woman."

"Is that what's got your hackles up? Was Tess a friend of yours?"

"I'm looking for Mason."

"Yeah, that's what I keep hearing," Hux said. "And just what do you plan to do to this Mason? You going to carve him up like you did those men at the river? Are you going to—"

Hux stopped, a sudden spark flickering in the back of his mind. He leaned forward, focusing on the stranger's face, chasing a faint call from somewhere in a distant part of his memory. He said, "Jesus, I know you."

"You don't."

"You're McCreary," Hux said. "Noah McCreary."

The stranger sat back, eyes suddenly hard and narrow. He stopped turning the coin.

"I was there," Hux said. "Good lord, man, is that what this is about? You think Zalen's group did it?"

"Did they?"

"No chance. They were out west at the time, been out there for years." Hux shook his head. "Make no mistake, Zalen's just the character to do such a thing. But it wasn't him; I can assure you of that."

"What were you doing there?"

"Passing through," Hux said, "reporting back to the army. It was over when I arrived, the whole place black and ruined. I had no idea what happened until I saw the man kneeling by that makeshift cross on that hill. It was while I watched that man that I knew."

McCreary looked away.

Hux said, "I heard the man on that hill lost his best friend that day. The kind one grows up with, plays with, learns about life with, the kind that can't be replaced. I felt sorry for that man then. I feel sorry for him still."

"What else did you hear?"

Hux shrugged. "Some said Indians; some said bushwhackers; one old fella said the gray man did it. A few said you did. But I knew it wasn't you. I knew that when I saw you on the hill."

McCreary's eyes came back to Hux. "Who's the gray man?"

"Hell if I know," Hux said. "Some old-timer mentioned that name to me in the next town over. He wouldn't say anything else, even when I pressed him. It was all the talk; nearly everywhere I stopped, people were talking about what happened in your little settlement. Except that old guy. I couldn't get anything else out of him."

McCreary was silent. Then: "You're Zalen's man?"

Hux nodded. "I guess I am."

"What does he want?"

"Right now? You."

"What else? Why are you in this town?"

"I don't know," Hux said, and immediately knew how pathetic it sounded.

"Why are you talking to me?" McCreary asked.

"Why not? You're going to kill me anyway, right?"

"Don't you deserve it?"

Hux took a breath. "I guess I do."

McCreary watched him a beat, as he had before. Then: "He sent you to this barn today?"

"Yes."

"Why?"

"To retrieve Theresa Reeves."

"For what?"

Hux let the silence stretch, hoping it would answer for him. Finally, he said, "You should know, McCreary. He won't stop. He'll hunt you 'till the end. And Moriya and Ashe ... let's just say you'd be wise to put that pistol in your mouth before they get ahold of you. And they will. They'll drive you. Such things are their purpose for being. It's what they're born to do.

"You've taken some men from him," Hux went on. "I'll give you that. But there's plenty more where they came from—*plenty*."

"I haven't met a man among you."

Hux nodded, swallowed. "Let's just get this over with, all right?"

McCreary stood and slipped the coin in his pocket. "The woman you had in this chair, the sheriff said you maimed her because of something he did."

"That was my instructions."

"But she wasn't maimed."

"I couldn't do it," Hux said.

McCreary walked around behind him, removing Hux's pistol as he passed. Hux put his head down and braced himself.

"Anything else?" McCreary asked.

"You figure it's too late to ask God for forgiveness?"

McCreary didn't answer.

Hux did anyway, a quick prayer his mother had taught him as a child.

He thought of his mom then, as he often did since she'd passed in his boyhood—how much he missed her, the security of simply laying his head on her chest. He remembered the sound of her voice through the fabric of her Sunday dress, a peace and safety that no gun, fort, or army had ever been able to replicate.

He thought it strange that such memories should surface at a time like this. Still, he wondered if he'd see her again, if the stories of the next life she'd told him were true. He hoped they were. And he hoped they weren't.

"Thank you for that," Hux said. And as he sat back and waited for the touch of cold steel on the back of his head, he said, "One request, if I may: let me face you. I want to see it coming. That's always been important to me."

Hux waited. And when no answer came, he slowly turned in his seat, resisting the urge to close his eyes in the face of his coming end.

McCreary wasn't there.

Hux wrestled with the idea of unhitching his horse, turning it west, and riding until the animal couldn't support him anymore. The impulse was pure, raw, and enticing, a deep instinct directing him toward nothing more than survival.

But he didn't. Nor did Zalen ask about the sheriff's wife or his three newest missing men when Hux arrived back in town. Instead, Zalen and Moriya were huddled in the back of the tavern, talking in whispers, as close as two opposing sides of magnets could be.

Several members of the group were standing at the front of the place—most of them, it fact. But none were drinking. None were talking.

Hux looked at Ashe and Ashe looked at him. The questions Hux feared passed over Ashe's face. But that was all. No words were exchanged. The whole place was as silent as a graveyard.

11

U S Marshal Jeremiah Perkins tugged on the reins and slowed his horse to a walk.

The wagon ahead sat leaning at a sharp angle on three wheels. Two dead lay sprawled at the rear of the rig facing southwest, no doubt where the men had tried to repel an attack from the hill above them. Another body lay partially obscured in the brush near the foot of the slope. This third one appeared to be a woman, judging by the tangled mess of cloth gathered around her legs.

The hem of a dress, Jeremiah thought. The sight and implications churned the acid in his stomach.

JEREMIAH and his party were still thirty minutes outside Cuttwood, so he was surprised to already see victims. He'd been told the gang, or whoever they were, had killed two deputy sheriffs upon entering the town and were threatening the same fate on the civilians.

The marshal had initially thought it an exaggeration—

who would do such a thing? But the source had been trust-worthy and the informant reliable, so he'd hastily thrown together a posse and struck out for the nearly two-day ride.

His party was seven-men strong, hard men, experienced in violence, easily the largest and most capable force he'd yet to assemble. And if the information he'd received was true, he figured he'd need every one of them.

Patrick Heller rode beside him, the only full-time deputy in the party—also the toughest and most fearless man Jeremiah had ever known. Like many men in the territory, Patrick had straddled the line between law and lawlessness. He'd also been a lifelong friend of Jeremiah's. So as soon as the opportunity arose, the marshal had been quick to pin a star on his friend's chest, out of the sure and terrible knowledge that if he didn't, Patrick would finish his days at the long end of a prison sentence, or a rope.

JEREMIAH LOOKED OVER AT PATRICK, who'd also slowed. The deputy was surveying the scene in front of them, quietly reconstructing the preceding events in the way only he could—maybe, Jeremiah thought with chagrin, from experience.

Patrick didn't speak during this process, nor did Jeremiah prompt him—not just because the marshal learned not to interrupt his friend during these moments, but also because that's when the woman's body moved.

Jeremiah immediately turned and signaled his remaining six men to hold. Then he quickly dismounted and approached the fallen woman.

Patrick said, "*Jeremiah* ..." but the marshal held up a hand and continued toward the woman.

Her chest was heaving and her body jolted when Jeremiah's shadow passed over her.

The marshal knelt and placed a hand on her shoulder. "It's okay now. No one's going to hurt you anymore."

"No more. Please no more."

"Easy now, ma'am. I'm a US Marshal and we're here to help."

Her eyes came to him, seemed to lose focus. She said, "Can't breathe. Can't get air."

Jeremiah turned and called out to Joseph Morrison, a man who'd briefly studied medicine back east before giving up the discipline for cards. He was the best they had.

The remaining men dismounted and began opening canteens and stretching their legs. A couple of them lit cigars.

The woman sat up as Morrison approached. She carefully surveyed the collection of deputies while pushing down the hem of her dress.

To Jeremiah, she said, "Thank you. That's much better."

Jeremiah noticed the Mexican accent for the first time. He also realized she seemed to be breathing better. He glanced back at Patrick, who looked at the wagon.

That's when the two dead men at the rear sat up, both holding pistols. The one closest to Jeremiah said, "Afternoon, Marshal."

Patrick shot the man in the head, startling everyone. Then he flicked his aim at the second man.

The rest of Jeremiah's men dropped what they were

doing and hurried back to their horses. Two of them had already drawn their rifles.

But it was too late. Nearly a dozen riders emerged over the crest of the hill, and still more from the woods at their rear—all hooded in burlap sacks, all firing their weapons, easily outnumbering Jeremiah's party two to one.

Jeremiah stood and drew his revolver. He had taken only a step before he felt the point of a knife at his throat.

The woman's voice behind him was pleasant now, measured but soft and tender. "Please release your weapon, Marshal."

"Damn you, woman. You have no idea what—" He felt the blade puncture his skin; a warm rivulet of blood streamed over his collarbone.

He dropped his pistol. All he could do now was watch.

Hux also watched, from a distance, marveling at the bravery of the marshal's men in what was obviously a forgone conclusion. But also at Ashe, who walked among the lawmen and hail of bullets like a devil of hell, methodically gunning down all who were near him, oblivious of the tightrope of death on which he was balanced.

Ashe's daring summoned a sense of both wonder and madness, and provoked feelings in Hux bordering on beauty, which he didn't understand or necessarily like.

The whole thing lasted no more than a minute, all of it well planned and executed. The classic damsel in distress. Another one as old as time.

Only the marshal survived the massacre. And only three group members had fallen.

. . .

IT TOOK some effort for the group to drag the marshal to the back of the ruined wagon, where they eventually stretched him out on his back and secured his arms and legs to the frame.

This part initially confused Hux—he'd been left out of the planning—until he saw the men back away and Moriya climb up beside the marshal.

The marshal struggled, pulled and jerked at the ropes.

Moriya knelt beside him. "You are a good man," she said in a soothing, almost maternal voice. "But your goodness has put you here."

Hux saw the marshal straining to look at his men. He also saw the tears in his eyes. The marshal said, "This day will return to you."

"Everything returns in time." Moriya opened his shirt and placed a hand on his chest, again comforting, gentle. She said, "Who sent for you?"

"Go to hell."

Moriya withdrew her knife and turned it around to catch the fading light.

The marshal's eyes never left his men.

"Your destination is the same, lawman," Moriya said. "So choose the easy path and you will find I am gentle and merciful. If you desire, your journey to peace can be as pleasant as lying down beside your woman for a long winter's sleep."

The marshal said nothing.

Moriya touched the knife against his bare flesh, dragged

the flat of the cool steel across his torso. She said, "Who sent for you?"

The marshal stiffened, but didn't reply.

Moriya nodded, and Hux watched her blade glide across the marshal's stomach, careful and meticulous, as though she were drawing a line—which she was, a red one.

The marshal passed out when she opened him up and began pulling things out of him and placing them on his chest. And so Moriya would rouse him before continuing her interrogation.

It was during the third awful cycle of this that Moriya received the answer to her question—one name, uttered in a pathetic whine, followed by, "God, forgive me."

It was the last words he spoke.

THE GROUP RETURNED to town in celebration, whooping and firing their weapons in the air. There were smiles and slaps on the back, and everything else Hux had seen victorious men do.

As they began dismounting, someone said, "Where's Hank and Karl?"

"Dragging ass like always," someone else said. "Probably already dippin' into Hank's flask!"

Another voice: "Can't let 'em get too far ahead of us!"

Laughter.

Hux swung down from his horse and looked back at the group. No Karl. No Hank. He glanced up and down the boardwalk, searched the street and dimming horizon.

And then, as the last few group members filed past him

into the tavern, Hux looked toward the south, where the sky was already the color of soot and ash.

He said, "Where's Moriya?"

MORIYA COULD SENSE the souls of Karl and Hank nearby, perhaps in limbo, perhaps trying to draw her attention. She was never sure which with the newly dead, just that they were there.

Their bodies were behind her now, lifeless and cooling beneath the ancient oak where they'd been slain. It was a beautiful tree, she thought, a peaceful place to die. Still, their souls were restless—of that, she was certain—and she suspected they yearned for retribution. Which was not hers to give, of course, nor was such a thing possible in this life.

The night had taken them without a sound, as was its way. They had performed well against the lawmen, no doubt attracting the attention of *el Coco*. And there was no questioning the judgment of *el Coco*, nor could the timid or faint of heart hope to resist him.

She dipped her hands in the cool river, using the moment not only to cleanse her body from the residue of the marshal's end, but also to clear and purify her mind, to wash away any unclean emotions that might pervert her mission.

When she was finished, when she felt her mind and body were clean and pure, she climbed up the riverbank and stood between the sun and moon.

She said, "I do not fear you, *el Coco*. I am happy to meet you, very glad you are here. Please allow me to look upon you."

Moriya wasn't surprised when the shadow stepped from the grove twenty yards distant.

She smiled. "It brings me great honor to see you in this form. It fills my spirit with pride. I recognize your mission has been just and righteous, as it always is, and I know my name is also on your list. Therefore, I know this will not be the last time we meet."

The shadow closed to ten yards.

Moriya drew her blade. The steel winked in the early moon. She said, "*Shhhh* ... let yourself be still. I sense your fatigue, the weight of the many souls you carry. Do not feel hesitant at your end, for we both know you will return only more glorious and powerful. Come to me now and allow me to release your burden. You will be pleased to find I am humble and worthy."

The shadow did.

OTTO CLINE WAS DRUNK, rehashing his old jokes and clapping men on the back. And tonight they were laughing. No more of the sullen or unimpressed looks. No more temper tantrums.

The mood in the group was markedly different tonight, now that something had gone their way. It was the way it had always been, the way it was supposed to be. Everything was back to normal.

Otto hadn't stopped drinking since learning about the fates of Cyrus and Quinn—which Zalen had allowed, and Otto was both surprised and grateful for.

He hadn't been allowed to take part in the ambush of the lawmen, however, which didn't necessarily bother him.

But the exclusion had earned him more than a few disapproving glares from the men, and that did bother him.

He staggered outside, stretched, yawned, nearly fell. He'd never heard of anyone being drunk for *days*, never thought such a thing possible. As he began relieving himself at the corner of the building, it struck him that he might have discovered his gift. Yeah, his *calling*. His father had always said everyone had one.

When he stepped back up on the boardwalk, everything began spinning again. So he stopped and leaned against the support post at the tavern entrance, pressed his cheek against its cool surface while the contents of his stomach sloshed, rose, and settled.

When everything stayed down this time—there couldn't be much left to come up, could there?—he looked up, blinked, and then narrowed his eyes at the stranger in the street, who was just standing there watching him.

"Oh, damn." Otto laughed. "Did I forget my britches again? Is that why you're staring at me?" He groaned, bent over, ran a hand down his legs and patted his knees. "*Naked again!*" he sang, nearly losing his balance. "*Naaay-ked boy!*"

But he wasn't naked. He felt the dirty, worn material of his pants between his fingers, checked his belt and buckle. All there.

He frowned, straightened, steadied himself. "You know it ain't polite to gawk at a man whilst ..." He stopped, squinted, shook his head, squinted again. "Hey, what the hell ..." Then: "Oh, Jesus."

That's when he went for his pistol. Which, of course, wasn't there.

· · ·

COMPARED to the one Hux had heard at the river, the scream this time was muted, or maybe cut short, because the men in the tavern continued drinking and carrying on like nothing had happened.

Except for the two men in the front, the pair leaning against the wall nearest the door. Hux watched as both men set down their drinks and turned an ear toward the sound.

The next cry, or whatever it was—Hux had heard nothing this time—must have triggered the two men. Because they both looked at each other, drew their weapons and rushed outside.

The second man immediately stumbled back in the door, choking and holding his throat, desperately trying to put back the scarlet flow of blood draining away between his fingers.

More screaming from outside, this time clearly audible. The first man.

The tavern fell silent and everyone turned and faced the front of the building.

Zalen leaned back in his seat, tapped his finger on the table, and said, "Open fire on that wall please."

Hux kept watching the man by the door. The guy backed against the wall, grasping his neck, retching and drowning in his own blood.

"Right now, Mr. Huxtable," Zalen said.

Hux nodded at the group members nearest him, and seven of them stood, raised their weapons, and opened up on the wall and door.

The gunfire was like a violent cannonade in the confined space, and powder smoke quickly filled the room.

The guy holding his throat went down immediately in a storm of lead, probably a mercy.

The force of the barrage shook the front wall and forced open the door—which promptly slammed again, Hux noticed. Had someone kicked it closed?

When the firing ceased, Zalen said, "Again, please."

Hux looked at him sharply, but Zalen simply covered his ears and stared ahead.

Hux's thoughts were on the first man who'd gone outside, and who was surely still on the walkway opposite the door, when the guns started up again without his prompting.

ALONG WITH OTTO CLINE, the first man was crumpled on the boardwalk when they opened what was left of the door. The reckless volleys had rendered him nearly unrecognizable, and Hux was bothered that he couldn't remember his name.

The bodies of both men also displayed the awful blade work Hux and the rest of the group had become familiar with.

Hux bent to close the men's eyes when Zalen said, "You see, my friends, it is just as I told you. He is simply a man. A spirit—*el Coco*—surely does not bleed."

Hux stepped off the boardwalk, following Zalen's eyes to the ground at his feet.

Blood. A lot of it. A thick, erratic crimson line in the dirt leading back up the street.

Hux knelt at a spot where the blood had pooled. "McCreary, you stubborn bastard, I warned you."

Behind him, Zalen said, "Please locate our wounded phantom, Mr. Ashner. Finish him off and put him in the ground."

Ashe started walking up the street.

Zalen turned to Hux. "We may begin casting the net now, Mr. Huxtable. Use the information the dear marshal provided and complete your mission. Now that our little insurgent is out of the way, even you should be able to manage that."

Hux tried to ignore the last part. But Zalen was right. The game had changed now. McCreary was hurt, probably hurt bad. And he was definitely off the board.

12

Hux hadn't been long in the group compared to some. Consequently, there were things he hadn't yet seen or experienced, or was only now experiencing—such as the method of interrogation used on the marshal, or Zalen's proclivity to place innocents against the wall.

What he also hadn't seen—and judging by the reaction of the men, no one else had either—was Zalen's silence.

Zalen hadn't spoken since they'd found Moriya's eviscerated body near the river. He hadn't issued orders, called for retribution, or lashed out in anger, which everyone seemed to be waiting for.

Zalen had kept his back to the group, his head occasionally tilting from the slow-moving river to Moriya's body and back again.

Even after they buried and left Moriya behind, he remained in that state the rest of the evening and night. In fact, Zalen didn't speak again until they located their quarry.

And this time he carried out the interrogation himself.

. . .

THE BOY TURNED when Zalen called out the name Luke Joyner, which immediately gave him away—the name the marshal had given up to Moriya and Ashe later delivered to Zalen.

And to Hux, he was a boy—too old to be considered a child, but still a distance away from manhood.

They intercepted him at his home as he was apparently packing to leave. His saddlebags were already stuffed and he was loading down a pack mule when the group arrived and surrounded the house.

The boy had shared the home with his father, whom, they'd learned from Otto, Cyrus had killed nights ago.

Luke Joyner took in the men cautiously. Yet, there was a knowing expression on his face that Hux wondered if anyone else recognized.

"Help you gentlemen?" the boy asked.

Zalen said, "You were planning a trip, young one."

Luke glanced at his horse. "I was just—"

Zalen hit him, a full-fisted punch that spun the boy around and left a cherry-red split at the corner of his mouth.

"That was not a question," Zalen said. "You will speak to me only when prompted."

To his credit, the boy quickly righted himself and rose to his full height, which brought him nearly nose-to-nose with Zalen. And while his eyes welled, there was fire in them too.

Hux admired the kid for that; he pitied him for it too.

"There exist only a few who know why I'm in your

town," Zalen said. "I, of course, am one of them. Two others are no longer with us. And if my deductions are correct, at least two more remain who also possess this knowledge."

Luke frowned, an expression of confusion.

"One of whom is still unknown to me," Zalen said. "The other, young one, is you."

Luke shook his head.

Zalen sighed. "Your actions have cost me much, child, much more than you're capable of repaying in your remaining life. I understand your father was a strong-willed man, and I see the beginnings of the same in you. Even facing the highest cost, he refused to reveal the information I seek."

Hux saw the boy's lips form the word *Father,* but he didn't speak it.

"But you will indulge me, child," Zalen said. "Whatever you believe now, your father was a coward. Like many, he has left the consequences of his behavior upon his offspring. And you will find, as I intend to show you, his indifference to pain and death does not reside in you."

Hux noticed Luke's hands, tucked at his sides, slowly clench into fists.

Zalen struck him again, a violent shot driving the boy to the ground. Zalen followed him down and delivered two more vicious blows. "You must strike when your instincts prompt you," he spoke into the boy's ear. "You must learn to ignore your inhibitions, for you never know when they will cost you everything."

Zalen rose and wiped his hands on his jacket. "I know you're the one who retrieved the marshal, Master Joyner.

Just like I know you are going to tell me where to find what I'm looking for."

Luke spat blood to the side. "I won't be telling you anything, mister."

Zalen grinned. "Ah, but you will, child. You will."

The boy started to get up, but Zalen kicked him in his ribs.

Zalen began in earnest then, beating the boy back into the dirt and then whipping him with his riding crop. "Do not whimper, boy! Only animals whimper! Act in such a way that you can be proud of your end."

On and on it went, over and over, the same question between each savage blow—"*Who was your father protecting? Who was your father protecting?*"

After what seemed like an hour but was likely only a few minutes, Zalen stopped and retrieved a shovel from the nearby porch, which he used to break the boy's leg and finally his will.

Hux said, "*Zee ...*"

Luke Joyner screamed out the answer then—which surprised Hux—and then began weeping bitterly.

That's when Zalen really started in on him.

When it was over, and he had the information he sought, Zalen stepped away from the bloody mess, produced a handkerchief and wiped his hands again. He looked to the south for a long time, a deep rumination in his eyes.

He said, "*Cooper.*"

.   .   .

NOAH MCCREARY FOUND the boy in the small hours of night. He'd followed the uniform line of tracks to the outskirts of the Joyner homestead, where they abruptly broke off into a pincer movement, enveloping the house.

The boy was only partly dressed and had obviously been beaten and tortured. A pair of spectacles, presumably belonging to the young man, were lying beside him, twisted and broken like their owner.

Noah knelt beside him. The boy had a small birthmark below his right eye, like a drop of red wine or a tear.

A whimper escaped him when Noah laid a hand on his shoulder.

"It's over now," Noah said.

"It hurts."

"I know. But not much longer."

And it wasn't. The boy only had the strength to utter two more words. He said, "*Piper*," first, which appeared to take the remaining spirit out of him.

And then, with what seemed his final bit of energy, he said, "*Mason*."

13

———————

Virginia leaned her shotgun against the wall and placed a hand on the counter. She'd tried flexing only her knees to get to the cabinets below, but couldn't manage it, couldn't help bending at the waist.

The nausea had dissipated after she'd thrown up twice, but the chills and lightheadedness were still coming and going. The lightheadedness was the worst.

"Mama?"

Virginia jolted at the sound of Piper's voice. She closed her eyes, took a breath, then gestured at the cabinet. "Fetch me the laudanum, would you?"

Piper knelt and looked through the space under the counter. "It's not in here. You have a headache or something?"

Virginia didn't answer. She started searching the drawers again, the same she'd already been through twice— or was it three times?

Piper said, "Are you leaving again?"

"No, baby."

Virginia picked up her shotgun and moved toward Bran and Piper's room.

Bran appeared in the doorway ahead of her. "Don't leave, Mama."

Virginia quickly touched her son's hair, told him to go back to sleep, then turned to wedge past him.

Bran clamped onto her with both arms and squeezed.

The explosion of pain tilted the room and brought bright orange flares swimming into her vision.

Bran backed away when she stiffened and cried out. He said, "Did I step on your toe?"

The nausea returned like a burning corkscrew through Virginia's throat and guts. She slumped against the door-jamb until the worst of it passed, then moved to the chair beside Piper's bed and sat down.

When the acid stilled and her vision cleared, she saw Piper and Bran filling the doorway to the bedroom.

Bran's eyes welled. "What's wrong, Mama?"

"I'm looking for the medicine."

Piper knelt in the doorway and picked up the shotgun Virginia had dropped.

"Don't handle that thing," Virginia said.

"What should I do with it?"

Virginia held up a hand. "*Just ... don't.*"

Piper laid the gun at her feet.

Virginia stared at the scattergun, blinked when it wavered in and out of focus.

Relax. Breathe. Focus.

She fumbled a match from her pocket, lit the candle on Piper's bedside table and opened the drawer. She must've left the medicine in here for some reason. Maybe she'd dropped it in the drawer when putting the children to bed. It *had* to be in here. She'd looked everywhere else.

It wasn't. Pencils and erasers. A paper clumsily tied around a dirty rock. Piper's favorite doll—a cloth and straw creation Virginia's father had made. No medicine bottle.

Virginia picked up the doll, ran a finger over the stitching, the crooked lips, uneven eyes and nose. She caressed the dark yarn on the doll's head, which was mostly gone. Dad had done his best. He always did his best.

Virginia placed the doll in the drawer and took out the crumpled paper, unwound the twine from around the dirty rock.

She sat back and scanned the worn, mud-stained page. And then scanned it again. Then she carefully read the first paragraph thoroughly, which took some time.

She looked up.

Piper was still in the doorway, her hand over her mouth. "I forgot about it."

Virginia said, "Where did you get this?"

"I'm sorry."

"Where?"

Piper told her. The river, the voices above them, the paper and rock, the sounds like thunder that probably wasn't. "I'm sorry, Mama. It's just with everything going on, I—"

Virginia held up a hand. "Fetch me the laudanum."

"Can you read it?" Piper asked.

"The medicine."

"What does it—"

"*Piper*!"

Her daughter left the room, tugging Bran behind her.

Virginia grimaced, adjusted her position on the chair, and went back to the letter, reading the page meticulously this time. It had been a long time since she'd seen the Latin alphabet, let alone tried to read anything written with it. And while the letters eventually formed the words her father had taught her, and the words sentences, paragraphs, and so on, there was still something missing, something she didn't understand.

She read it again, and then again.

It wasn't until she finished her fifth pass of the letter, and leaned back in her chair, that she noticed the man standing inside the room with her.

THE MAN EASED the door closed and sat down in the chair beside the wall. He nodded at the shotgun. "Kick it over here."

Virginia didn't move. For a long moment she watched him watching her, his hands resting across one another on his lap, his right close to the grip of his pistol, which he carried cross-draw. He didn't look away, didn't blink.

Virginia nudged the shotgun toward him with the toe of her boot.

"Now the blade," he said.

"Why would I do that?"

The man tilted his head in the direction of the children, who were in the next room. "Because you have something to live for."

Again Virginia studied him. He still hadn't drawn his weapon, still hadn't made a threatening move.

She began calculating the distance between them, the

steps it would take to get there—*one-two-three*—the pain she'd have to endure, or ignore, the effort it would take to get out of the chair.

The man said, "You can't make it."

She slipped a hand around the small of her back, closed her fingers around her knife. "You won't be getting near my children."

"I'm not interested in your children."

"Then state your intentions."

"I'm looking for Mason."

Virginia stiffened at the name. Something cold broke and swam through her chest and back. Her grip tightened around the blade.

He said, "Where were you in seventy-nine?"

"Here."

"*Don't lie to me.*"

Virginia blinked at the change in his voice. "I'm not. I swear it. The sheriff, anyone in town, will tell you the same; anyone who's left."

"Your husband?"

"Out west. He's dead now."

The man went silent. And the discomfort she experienced as his eyes dipped into her—reached and probed and searched—surprised and startled her.

His eyes were soft and round and tired, but also possessed a restrained black malice that made her skin prickle. They were hatred. They were compassion. They were the two warring against each other.

She said, "You're him, aren't you?"

The man didn't answer.

"I know about you," Virginia said. "I know what you

did for Sally White Horse, and I know what you did for me, and I'm much obliged."

The man looked away, the first time he'd broken eye contact.

"I didn't know they were there until I was past the livery stable," Virginia said. "It was reckless to go into town that night. I'm in your debt."

"I don't reckon you needed any help."

"You don't know them then, mister. You don't know what they would've done to me, or my children once I was out of the way."

The man said nothing.

"Life means nothing to them," Virginia said, "not mine, not yours, not even their own. Their leader can't see anything beyond his current obsession, and his followers will stop at nothing to bring that desire to him."

"Why?"

Virginia leaned forward. "Because he enlists demons in his group, not people. And if they're not demons in the beginning, he converts them, molds them, or disposes of them. He wants there to be no scenario which his group can't handle, and no qualms over ends justifying means."

"Is that why you've been killing them?"

Virginia sat back, relaxed her grip on the knife. "I had no choice. They threatened my babies. Given the chance, they'd kill everyone in this house, or worse."

The man's eyes came back to her. "Children? What makes you think they'd go that far?"

The tears came then. Though she tried, Virginia couldn't restrain them any longer.

She said, "Because I'm one of them."

. . .

Zalen said, "Given your military *expertise*, how do you suggest we proceed?"

Even as he asked, Zalen's eyes never strayed from the south, just as they hadn't since leaving the Joyner homestead. Hux ignored the sarcastic way he used the word *expertise*.

Zalen had directed the group to ready their weapons, check their mounts and supplies of ammo, which everyone had done in an orderly fashion. The mood, Hux noticed, wasn't far removed from his stay in the army. Some of the men even slipped into the burlap hoods, as if donning uniforms.

"Go directly at them," Hux said. "I mean, it's a woman, two children, and a simpleton. They can't even mount a defense. But I don't understand why—"

Zalen swung his horse around and held up a hand to silence him. "There is much you do not understand, Mr. Huxtable."

Zalen approached the group and raised his voice. "Cyrus and Quinn. Amos and Gavin. Karl and Hank. Otto and Toby. Emery and ... *Moriya*."

He turned his horse in front of the group, eyes stopping briefly on each man. "Your comrades. Your friends. Your fellow warriors. Dead."

Murmurs and nods, curses and groans.

"And contrary to what some of you think," Zalen said, "the killer of our comrades is not a spirit, but nor is it a man." He paused. "Our *el Coco* is a woman, flesh and bone, tissue and blood. She has children and no doubt possesses troubles common to all of her gender. But she is also the most deadly being I have ever known."

More grumbling among the group. Someone on the end laughed and spat.

Zalen tilted his head toward the man. "This woman has defied death more times than I can remember. And if you don't treat this as a fight against Lucifer himself, then she will sidestep the grave again and put you in her place. That, dear friend, I guarantee."

Zalen let the statement sink in. Then: "She uses her femininity as a disguise, camouflage. Just like I taught her. And when you near her lair she wields her lovely little blade like the tooth and claw of a lioness. Given the chance, she will devour every one of you and leave you to the scavengers. *Just. Like. I. Taught. Her.*"

Silence.

Zalen turned to Hux. "Her name is Audrey Mason. And she is my greatest creation."

Hux glanced to the east, where daylight was nudging the horizon. "Audrey Mason? I thought she was dead."

"So did I," Zalen said. He turned back toward the south. "And now we shall proceed to take her apart, Mr. Huxtable, piece by delicate little piece."

THE MAN's hand moved toward his pistol.

Virginia let go of her blade and held her hands in front of her. "It was years ago. I went by Audrey back then, my middle name. My married name was Mason. I dropped both when I came back home."

The man tapped the grip of his revolver. "And they just let you walk away?"

Virginia lifted the hair from her forehead, revealing her scar. "We were ambushed. Someone tipped the local marshal of our whereabouts and I was shot in the head during the exchange.

"The group was small back then," she said. "They left me behind because they thought I was dead. *I* thought I was dead, until I looked up and saw Tess cleaning the blood out of my eyes. She was the only one who came back for me. She was ... *Oh, Tess.*"

"Why didn't you go back to them?"

"My babies. I was thirteen when I followed Landry out west and got married. But I was a child. I never wanted that life. We were hungry and poor and tired and ready to give up before we met Zee. He told us he could lift us out of our poverty. He said he could show us the path to our dreams, the life we really wanted."

Virginia shook her head. "He was so damn persuasive. He made everything sound so good, so easy. At first it was simple robberies, no one got hurt, but in time it became like riding with the devil of hell. I had no idea what was happening to me until it was too late. I didn't know what I'd become until I looked at my daughter's perfect newborn eyes and saw my bloodstained hands cradled beneath her. Everything changed then. The whole world became different."

Virginia touched her scar. "The bullet hit me like a hammer that day, but it turned out to be the greatest gift I've ever received." She met the man's eyes. "Don't you see? Suddenly there was a way to give my children a chance, to get them away from the violence and give them a life, a chance to become who they really are. And it worked. I got away while my daughter was still too young to remember, and I was still pregnant with my son."

"You think that makes what you did okay?"

"No," Virginia said, surprised by the crack in her voice. "It doesn't. But children shouldn't have to pay for the sins of their parents, should they? Even then I knew I didn't deserve an escape, but they did."

"You ever think of those who didn't escape, those who you took the world from?"

"I never killed a child. I wouldn't."

"Everyone is someone's child."

Virginia frowned, nodded. "I know I'll pay for the things I did back then. I know there'll be a reckoning."

"This Tess, she was a friend of yours?"

"My best friend," Virginia said. "She saved my life that day, more than she'll ever know. If it hadn't been for her, I expect the lawmen would've discovered me alive, dragged me through the street and hanged me. And God only knows what would've become of Piper."

Virginia shook her head and glanced at the letter. "If I had known Tess was in one of those shallow graves they left up on the ridge ..."

She withdrew the tobacco and paper from her coat and began trying to roll a cigarette with trembling hands.

"Tess was the only one of us who had a code back then," she said. "She was probably the only one of us who had a soul. Aside from Ephraim, she was also the only one who knew I was still alive and who I really am."

"Your husband left you behind too?"

Virginia lit the cigarette, but the fire and loose tobacco dropped off in the floor. She retrieved some fresh paper and started over.

"He said he'd meet me here, that we'd start over, start anew. But I watched the gate for years and he never came. He'd send letters from time to time, always saying he was going to make everything right. But eventually the letters stopped coming and somehow I knew."

Virginia held up the letter. "I know he's dead now. Tess killed him, says she was doing him a favor. She says he stole this and Zalen was hunting him for it. Tess got to him before the group and shot him in an act of mercy. She says he was wounded and couldn't travel so she offered him the charity, because if Zalen had found him first ... well, I'm sure you can imagine."

She tossed the letter to him. "She says Landry wanted me to have this. But I don't understand why? Except to tell me he was dead, I don't know why he'd want Tess to come all this way to deliver a letter."

The man picked up the page but only glanced at it. He leaned back in his chair. "You don't know what that is, do you?"

"It's Latin. My father taught me—"

The man shook his head, nodded at the bedside table.

Virginia glanced at the open drawer—Piper's doll, her pencils, paper, and erasers, the rock Tess's letter had been wrapped around.

"I don't ..." Virginia stopped. The rock. Dirty and stained. The size of her fist. But here and there, in the glow of the candle, a glint of yellow, a vein of gold reflecting in the soft light.

"Yes."

Virginia stared at the door. A tear dropped off her cheek. She said, "Are you leaving?"

Noah met her eyes one last time. Then he kicked the shotgun back to her, turned and walked out.

14

_____

The group assembled into a loose skirmish line after crossing the bridge, rifles and shotguns across their laps, the last man just joining with news that Ashe was on his way.

The formation surprised Hux because it was aggressive and more or less what he'd suggested.

Surprising him more, however, was the last man to join the line.

After speaking with Zalen, Elias fell in beside Hux at the rear.

"Bastard snuck up behind me," the old scout said, "snatched my pistol, and stabbed my horse in the flank. Took damn near the whole day to calm that pony and walk it back in, but not before I went for one hell of a ride. Got a better look at those mountains to the north, though. Always have been enchanted by them hills."

Hux said, "You're lucky he didn't—"

"I know."

Just before the Cooper homestead came into view,

Zalen signaled for the two men to break off toward the woods where the river fed in from the northwest. "Bring those children out please."

Hux said, "Why'd you come back?"

Elias looked at him. "I told you not to ask me that again."

Virginia didn't hear Noah leave, not the door closing, or horse's hooves, or anything else. Neither did she notice the first weak rays of sunlight illuminating the bedroom window or the intense quiet in the house. She didn't hear, feel, or sense anything at all, until the touch of her daughter's hand was on her shoulder.

"I have the medicine," Piper said.

Virginia raised her head, bit her bottom lip. "Thank you."

"Did that man make you cry?"

Virginia shook her head. "Headache, like you guessed."

"Bad one, huh?"

"Bad one."

Virginia took the laudanum from Piper and turned it around in her hand. She tightened her fingers around the cork, then let go and set the bottle on the bedside table.

She saw Piper staring at the shotgun again.

"Where's Cotton?" Virginia asked.

Piper pointed toward the adjoining room. "Sitting by the window."

"This whole time?"

"Just came inside."

Virginia stood. The room tilted as it had when Bran

hugged her, causing her to place a hand on the wall, but not as violently this time.

"You oughta lay down," Piper said.

Virginia blinked, said, "I've got to ... I've ..." She placed an arm on her daughter's shoulder. "Come with me, baby."

BRAN AND COTTON were playing checkers beneath the corner window.

Bran pointed at the board. "Move that one there."

Cotton's brow furrowed as he studied the pieces. He placed a finger on the one Bran suggested, then moved another.

Bran sighed, glanced back at Virginia and Piper. "I can't beat nobody."

"Cotton."

The big man looked up at the sound of Virginia's voice. He slid away from the game board and stood.

"Take the kids out back," she said, "to that hidden path you like to use, then circle around toward the ridge."

Piper looked at her. Bran did too.

"Get to the woods," Virginia went on. "Then follow the river to Ephraim's place and wait for Luke. He'll help you get to ..." She paused.

"Get to where?" Piper asked.

"Luke will know a place. Just tell him I sent you to find a place."

"What if Luke's not there?"

Virginia didn't answer, because she didn't know.

"But where will you be?" Bran asked. "When will you get there?"

"I'll catch up. But don't wait for me."

Bran looked away, confused. Virginia placed her fingers on his cheek, gently brought his face back to hers. "You'll be okay, *but don't wait for me.*"

Bran frowned. His eyes flicked over her shoulder. "Is it those men that's scaring you?"

Virginia glanced back at the window. Several riders, two dismounted and opening the gate. They were already here.

Cotton also turned toward the window.

"Are those the bad men from that night?" Bran asked.

Virginia instinctively moved to secure the door, but thought better of it.

"Audrey Mason!"

The voice echoed through the house like a roll of thunder before a storm, or, for Virginia, like the dead reaching up from the grave.

Piper said, "Who's that, Mama?"

"A man I used to know."

"No, who's he calling for?"

Virginia said, "It's time to go, Cotton."

Cotton was still looking out the window.

"Cotton!"

The big man turned.

"Don't let them see you," she said, "any of you."

Cotton looked back at the window, then back to Virginia.

"Go," Virginia said.

They did, all of them. Just like that, the house was empty. And not just physically. The place seemed hollow now, an indescribable void Virginia somehow knew would never again be displaced.

The realization hit her like a sickness—the return of sins hoped forgotten, the consequences of a teenage girl's decisions, the reaper come for harvest.

She leaned against the wall, searched her mind for her father again, his exhausted bedside voice when the nighttime terrors gripped her as a child. They sometimes gripped her still.

She whispered, "'The Lord is my shepherd; I shall not want ...'"

The words of the psalm immediately flooded her with feelings of longing, regret, and hypocrisy. A world that had passed and not passed, near enough to touch, taste, or feel, but also as distant and inaccessible as the moon and stars.

"Audrey Mason!"

"'He maketh me to lie down in green pastures; he leadeth me beside the still waters ...'" She laid her head against the door. She couldn't remember the rest of it. It was there, she knew, but hiding from her like she'd hidden from it.

She inhaled and exhaled, tried to clear her mind. And when she was satisfied enough time had passed, she stood back and faced the door, flinching at the pain, which was now slicing through her hip and leg like tongues of fire.

But the worst was coming from a deeper place, the place where joys and hurts are stored and compounded, the place that resists everything and nothing, never heals when injured, and never ever forgets.

Virginia focused on the physical pain, the only kind she could hope to control. She drew it in, held it, and released it, just like she'd learned years ago.

Then she opened the door.

·   ·   ·

NOAH MCCREARY RECROSSED the river in the place he had hours ago, the same shallow water he'd observed the five men wade through nights before, well down from the bridge.

Even from a distance, he'd heard those five men talking that night, heard what they'd planned for the small family in the valley. And then, like now, he'd reminded himself not to care.

He paused on the bank and watched the river slipping past, waited for that ephemeral call he'd come to rely on, that preternatural draw toward his daughter he'd both nurtured and blindly trusted these last three years—the same that had given him nothing in return.

It was there, the feeling, but quiet and distant, impossible to interpret. And although he understood the cause of this anomaly, he again reminded himself not to care.

"I've been looking for you."

Noah didn't bother turning in the direction of the voice, didn't lift his head or eyes. He just continued to focus on the water, which seemed to be speaking to him in a way he couldn't understand. He said, "You're not very good at it."

"You should ready your weapon in unfriendly territory."

It was the one they called Ashe. The man had already drawn his rifle from its saddle boot and had it resting across his lap. Noah noticed that detail minutes ago when Ashe emerged from the trees to the north.

"Leaving already?" Ashe prompted. "Aren't you curious to see what we'll do to the bitch and her pups?"

Noah said nothing.

"Don't you wonder what price she'll pay for her treachery?"

Noah didn't answer.

Silence.

Ashe said, "The man you killed in that alley was a friend."

"You should pick better friends."

"I don't choose my friends."

Noah said nothing.

Ashe moved closer. "You should've readied your weapon."

Noah looked up from the river. "You should've raised that rifle."

Hux watched Virginia Cooper step off the front porch and approach the line of men. The strap of her shotgun was looped over her shoulder, the same piece he'd taken from her just days before, and there was a slight hitch in her otherwise determined stride.

She looked tired, too, and pale, also older than he remembered. In fact, he'd thought her too young to have a child her daughter's age when he'd first seen her. Not today.

She stopped in front of the group and tossed a rock at the hooves of Zalen's horse.

"Take it and go," she said. "I had no part in it."

"Audrey," Zalen said. "I believed you dead."

"Audrey is dead."

"Shot in the head," Zalen went on, "saw it with my own eyes. But yet here you are, right as rain. How can that be?"

"It was a graze, a lot of blood."

"A graze ..." Zalen seemed to chew on the word. Then: "Did you know I had the man who shot you hunted down and killed?"

Virginia shook her head.

"Loyalty, Audrey. I was always loyal to you, just as I promised. Yet you deserted me, never even said goodbye. Why?"

"I had a child, Zee."

"Ah, yes. A child. And where is your young daughter? I think I should like to see her. Does she resemble her mother? I do hope she didn't inherit her father's—"

"She's dead," Virginia said. "Died years ago with the fever."

Virginia glanced at Hux then, just a quick flick of her eyes.

Hux looked away.

"Yes, dear Audrey," Zalen said. "Mr. Huxtable has told us of your young family, your daughter *and* son. Tell me: what is your boy's name?"

"I had no part in this."

Zalen frowned. "No part? Did you have no part in the deaths of our comrades?" He gestured at the men around him. "And the woman you killed, did you take her from the shadows? Did you draw her into one of your lovely traps?"

"We met face to face."

"And?"

"She was good."

"Indeed," Zalen said, nodding. "Apparently not good enough, though."

Virginia said nothing.

Zalen raised four fingers and four men dismounted and slowly began encircling her. He said, "You remember what happens now, don't you?"

Virginia slid back a step. "I had no part in this."

"So you say. But surely you haven't forgotten the price for killing a member of the group?"

"They threatened my children."

"Yes, yes," Zalen said. "Your fate pains me too. It truly does. Cyrus, Quinn—though I reject it, I understand your maternal instincts with them. But why the others? Why enter a contest you knew you could not win?"

Virginia's eyes flared. "To bring you out of your hole."

Hux shook his head. What was she doing? Was she suicidal? Did she want to die? Then it hit him: yes, she did; she was stalling, buying time.

He glanced over his shoulder where the river curved back toward the north, where Zalen had dispatched the two men, where the Cooper children were no doubt hiding.

Zalen looked down at the rock for the first time. "I believe Tess would be disappointed in you, Audrey. Bringing that here cost her everything, yet you freely toss it aside."

Virginia didn't respond. She was watching the approaching men now, two on either side.

"If you wish to avoid this part," Zalen said, "you may simply relinquish your weapon. I am sure you recall how unpleasant this first stage can be."

Hux saw Virginia's shoulders relax, saw the strap of the shotgun inch down her arm.

The men moved closer.

"No?" Zalen said, rubbing his hands together. "Let us begin, then."

The men spread out and stopped, the encircling maneuver becoming a box—one man on each corner, Virginia in the center—which Hux thought was smart of the men, given she only had two rounds in the shotgun.

The man to her immediate right said, "Come now, little lady, ain't no need to be antsy. Just allow that scattergun to slide off your arm. We'll collect it and no harm'll come to you. Got my word on it."

He smiled reassuringly and extended a hand—pretty convincing, Hux thought.

The man's smiled widened when Virginia angled her head toward him, seeming to consider his proposition. Then he stepped back and broke into laughter, "Stupid bitch!" and the two men to her left rushed her.

They came at her hard and fast, hands and fingers extended like grappling hooks, both of them focused on immobilizing her, getting her on the ground, getting the shotgun.

And both died instantly and horribly when Virginia pivoted, dropped to a knee, and opened up both barrels of her weapon, close range, one for each of them.

The move froze the men to her right, and Virginia already had two more shells in her hand. She snapped open the breach, removed the empty loads, fumbled and dropped one of the fresh cartridges, and slid the other one home.

The men quickly recovered, knocking the shotgun from her hands just as she swung it around and pulled the trigger.

The ill-aimed buckshot caught Elias in the shoulder,

knocking him off his horse.

Virginia stabbed the third man in the chest with a knife that appeared from nowhere. The man stumbled back with a shocked expression on his face, and then dropped and fell, taking the blade with him.

The surviving fourth man grabbed the barrel of her shotgun and threw a savage elbow into her mouth.

The blow stunned her and she staggered back.

Two more men quickly dismounted and tackled her, cursing, yelling, swinging their fists.

The first blows took Virginia in the face, slapping her head against the ground; then they started on her ribs.

Virginia struggled, kicked, caught one man in his stomach, and then reached around her back for something that wasn't there.

Another two men joined in. The first delivering a running boot to her hip, eliciting a scream from her that shook Hux to his marrow. The second man swung the stock of his rifle, connecting flush with the back of her head.

Virginia rolled to her stomach, blinked, blinked again. A line of blood stretched and broke from her lower lip. As she began pushing herself up the man behind her kicked her above the ear.

Virginia Cooper went still.

"Hold," Zalen said.

The men stopped.

"Lift her, please."

They jerked her up by the back of her head. Her face was red and swelling, blood weeping from above her left eye and down her chin from her lower lip.

"Your skills were never very effective in the open," Zalen said. "It's a shame we never completed your training."

Hux looked at the three dead men, then Zalen.

"Very well," Zalen said, removing his riding crop. "Shall we move to the next step?"

Silence.

"Are you still with us, Audrey?"

Virginia said nothing. Hux wasn't sure she could.

Zalen said, "Rouse her, please."

One of the men spat on her, then another. A third backhanded her.

Virginia was quiet.

The men leaned toward her again but stopped when someone said, "Ashe is here."

Hux glanced back and saw Ashe's unmistakable brown and white paint horse approaching from the north. He felt the anticipation rise in the group like a physical force.

Elias sat up, inspected his wounded shoulder, and said, "Damn."

The group began backing away long before Ashe reached the gate, those nearest to Zalen parting to allow his assassin to pass through.

Which he did.

15

V irginia's world was alternating light and dark. She
felt fingers grip the back of her head, felt them dragging her up by her hair. She felt a warm mist on the side of
her face, an angry bite on her cheek, and the sharp angle of a
boot heel in her back.

But it was all general and displaced, a gentle pressure or
light tickle on numb skin.

Her father had said that was God's way of easing the
pain. He'd said that after she'd fallen out of a tree and
twisted her ankle, the same tree he'd told her never to climb
—not the last time she would fall.

Her father again.

She knew she should've killed Zalen first, knew it was
the right move. Her instincts had been *screaming* at her to
do just that. And she could've. It would've been easy.

But it was also the wrong move. Every moment she
stayed alive was another step for Piper, Bran, and Cotton,
another breath and second of hope. And if she had killed

Zalen, the remaining members of the group would've overwhelmed her and put her down immediately.

Zalen wouldn't do that, she knew. Zalen wanted her to suffer. He wanted to drag this out, make it last, make her hurt. And that's what she wanted too. She was prepared to suffer. She was ready to stand, and when she couldn't stand, to breathe, and when she couldn't breathe ...

That hope drained away, however, when the brown and white paint emerged and took its place beside Zalen.

She'd seen the rider of this horse, seen the cold rage in his eyes—and the absence of anything else.

Virginia knew it was over then, knew her time was up. This man would not toy with her. This man would end it.

Hux saw something drain from Virginia Cooper when Ashe's horse stopped beside Zalen. He saw the determination in her eyes diminish. He saw disappointment, resignation, and maybe fear.

But when she lifted a hand and smeared the blood away to clear her vision, Hux saw another change. He saw confusion.

Those who already had weapons in hand swiveled and adjusted their aim. Those who weren't carrying a rifle or hadn't yet drawn their sidearm did so.

But that was all.

Like Virginia, everyone in the group was suddenly unsure, silent, and very still—every man of them, Hux included.

Even as Zalen chastised Audrey over her treachery,

lectured her on her fate and how she'd brought this condemnation on herself, the men sat motionless, fidgety.

Even when Noah McCreary pressed the tip of his blade into the side of Zalen's neck, no one made a move to stop him. No one knew how to.

McCreary leaned close to Zalen. He said, "Lower your head when you speak to her."

Zalen tried to turn, but the pressure from the blade prevented him. "Well, it appears an ally has arrived, Audrey. But I must say—"

"I said, *lower your head when you speak to her*." McCreary's voice was gravel and ice.

Hux saw the tip of McCreary's knife loose a trickle of blood above Zalen's collar.

Zalen didn't lower his head. He said, "I see you have taken my man's horse."

"I took more than that."

"And what now? You propose to kill us all with a knife?"

Two men laughed, but the laughter was forced and lacked conviction.

McCreary said, "Just you."

"Ah, but it will not be just me, will it? Because as soon as you thrust your blade my friends here will cut you down. And then, with or without me, they will proceed to do the same with her"—Zalen gestured at Virginia—"but slowly, as they've been instructed. I assure you, stranger, they *will* complete their mission."

Noah glanced at the men, the first time he'd done so.

"Are you willing to die needlessly for this woman?"

Zalen asked. "To add an additional thirty seconds to her life?"

"There's not enough of you."

Zalen's eyes flicked to the dead men, then to the remaining group members he could see. "Not enough? You consider seven-to-one favorable odds?"

"You don't have seven men."

Hux expected McCreary to try something then, maybe whirl and fire at someone, attempt to even things up. But he didn't. He kept the knife at Zalen's neck.

"I shall make you an offer, stranger," Zalen said, "a onetime reprieve from your egregious error. You are clearly out of your depth and this matter doesn't concern you. So if you leave your weapons on the ground before me and withdraw now, I will allow you to ride away without pursuit."

"I am going to ride away," McCreary said.

Zalen's jaw flexed. Blood rushed pink into his cheeks and neck. "Mr. Huxtable!"

"Yes?"

"Kill this man! And when he and I fall, make this woman suffer like none have suffered before. Disable her and then start on her children. Make them scream and make her watch. And, Mr. Huxtable, under no circumstances are you to allow this woman to take her own life before her offspring's ends are complete."

McCreary's attention drifted to Virginia—Virginia, the house, Virginia, then the forest to the west. His eyes narrowed.

Zalen grinned, sensing his unease. "That's right, stranger. You were hasty showing your hand, an amateur's mistake. We already have her offspring, and even if they're still alive there's nothing you can do for them now."

An animal whine escaped Virginia and she tried to rise, but the men held her down.

McCreary said nothing.

Zalen said, "Do you understand my instructions, Mr. Huxtable?"

"I do."

"I trust you will see this through to the end."

"I will."

"Good man," Zalen said. "Proceed, then."

Hux swung his rifle around, took aim and breathed out to steady his hands. He peered down the sights, saw McCreary mouth the word *run* to Virginia, saw his free hand move toward his holstered pistol.

And then everything slowed, narrowed. Then there was only the soft flesh above the right ear, a place of maximum vulnerability, a place where a beating heart could mysteriously be seen and felt, and easily extinguished. A place that would never, nor could ever, deflect a bullet.

A kill shot every time.

Zalen said, "Fire, Mr. Huxtable."

Hux did. A tremor rose from his horse, throwing his aim off an inch or two. But the shot was true enough, the bullet striking Zalen just left of his right eye, snapping his head to the side and dropping him in a heap at his horse's hooves.

Stillness and silence, only the rifle's echo reverberating and fading through the surrounding trees.

No one moved. No one spoke.

Virginia blinked, wiped her eyes.

The men holding her let go.

Hux lowered his rifle. To the group, he said, "It's over."

But it wasn't.

PIPER JUMPED when she heard the gunshots, literally leapt in place. A cacophony of explosions: one, a pause, then *one-two-three-four-five*, each immediately following the other, the last two overlapping. She and Bran began running then.

They'd become separated from Cotton since entering the woods. Which was okay. Piper didn't need his help getting to Ephraim's anyway, and she sure as the world didn't trust him. Still, this area of the woods was largely new to her, and though she knew they only needed to find the river, and she was confident she could do just that, she wasn't entirely sure it was the right thing to do.

And she was mad, mad at Cotton, mad at her mom, mad at the man who'd made her mom cry, mad at the men who'd upended their lives—*mad-mad-mad*!

But she was scared too. The footsteps she'd been hearing for the past several minutes were getting closer. And they didn't belong to Cotton, she knew, because there were two sets of them.

Another gun shot went off, this one so close Piper felt as much as heard it. She glanced over her shoulder and nearly tripped over her younger brother, who'd been running in front of her.

That's when Bran went down and started chanting, "*If I'm still, it'll pass by; If I'm still, it'll—*"

Piper snatched him up by the shoulders. "Bran, we ain't got time for—"

Bran went right back down. "*If I'm still, it'll pass by; If I'm still—*"

Piper grabbed him and he kicked her. She reached for him again and he scratched her arm and tried to bite her.

"Bran!"

Her brother raised his voice, still chanting, now almost yelling the mantra.

Piper ground her teeth and looked away.

She saw the carvings then. The tiny house had been knocked off its base when Bran dropped to the ground, or maybe he'd fallen over it. She'd briefly registered the thing while trying to get Bran back on his feet, but dismissed it as just another chunk of broken wood—which, in a sense, it was.

But it was also an exact replica of their home, down to the pillars and rocking chairs on the front porch. Only now it was resting on its side. Several smaller carvings were still standing beside it, though, still positioned where the front of the house should've been. Four people: a woman, a girl, a boy and man. The man was a good bit larger than the other three, and he wasn't standing near as close as the woman and two children, but he wasn't far from them either.

The carvings' detail was exquisite and familiar, and Piper immediately knew by whose hand they'd been created.

She picked up the figurine with her likeness, suddenly fascinated by it, careful not to break the smaller, more fragile pieces. She let it roll into her palm, marveling at the detail of the figure's dress, the part in its hair. She'd just flipped it over when a boot appeared from nowhere, kicking it from her hand and sweeping away the rest.

Piper whirled in time to see the same boot coming at her, connecting flush with her chest, blasting the air from her lungs and toppling her backward into Bran.

The strange man kicked away the carving of the house. "Playin' with your dolls, huh, little lady? Now, ain't that sweet."

Piper grasped her chest, which suddenly seemed dead and unable to receive air. She reached behind her, tried to shove Bran away, tried to tell him to run, but she couldn't make the words come out.

The man stepped on her ankle and twisted his boot.

Piper screamed. And this time she was able to produce sound, though it was scarcely more than a whine.

"Shut up, boy," the man said.

Bran kept chanting, and even though she couldn't see him, Piper knew his eyes were pinched closed and he was covering his ears.

"I said, quiet!"

Bran got louder.

"Come on out, Manny," the man called over his shoulder. "And stop firing that pistol, for God's sake. You might hit somebody!"

The man stood over Piper, straddling her, big, tall, and muscled, long heavy beard. He drew his revolver and aimed it at Bran.

"I ain't going to say it again, boy."

Piper's voice returned. "Bran!"

"Can't be very heavy, that one," the man said. "So it'll

be your job to drag him back to your mama when we're through here."

"Run, Bran!" Piper began kicking the man's leg, his calf and shin, and then angled her aim for the side of his knee.

But his boot clamped over her ankle again, pinning and locking her foot beneath it. The pain was incredible, and she thrashed and screamed and flung a rock at the man.

The man steadied his revolver, rocked the hammer back.

And then he began rising off the ground, literally hovering above the earth before her like something from another world. His eyes went wide and his mouth opened in a silent O.

His feet dangled, kicked, and jerked, and his pistol dropped into the leaves. Then his head snapped to the side, a quick, unnatural jerk to the left, followed by a soft internal pop.

The man fell across Piper's legs and she scrambled out from under him. She touched her ankle and winced, and then looked up at Cotton, who was standing where the man had been.

Cotton looked at her, too, her ankle and leg, the muddy boot print on her dress, the dirt and leaves clinging to her hair and face. Then he knelt and set about reorganizing the tiny wooden house and figurines.

Piper glanced in the direction where the man had called to his friend. But the woods were still and quiet. The man called Manny never appeared.

Bran went on chanting.

. . .

HUX ROLLED OVER. At first, he couldn't see or hear anything through the haze of powder smoke and the intense ringing in his ears.

There was pain, too, coming and going, his leg partly numb and partly throbbing where his horse had come down on it. He could move it, though, and hoped that was a sign nothing was broken.

He'd seen McCreary slide off his saddle like liquid, seen him disappear among the mounted group members. He'd seen the men turning, yelling, firing wildly. He'd seen two of them fall.

And then Hux was on the ground, thrown from his horse. And a heartbeat later, everyone else was down as well.

Everyone except Noah McCreary, who, as Hux's vision cleared, was standing over Elias.

Elias looked up at him and sighed. He let go of his injured shoulder and slipped his hand over his pistol. "All right, stranger. Reckon it's as good a day to die as any."

McCreary tapped the grip of his revolver. "Whatever suits you."

"Wait, McCreary," Hux said. "We're leaving, me and him. Been itching to see those mountains to the north. Figure it's a good time to make the trip."

"Is that all you're itching to do?"

"That's all. I swear it."

McCreary angled his head toward Hux. "Folks change their mind."

Hux held up a hand. "I've already changed mine."

McCreary looked at Elias.

Elias let go of his pistol.

McCreary walked over to Ashe's horse and drew the

Henry rifle from its scabbard. As he turned and started toward the woods, Hux called out, "How'd you know I wouldn't fire on you?"

McCreary kept walking.

VIRGINIA STARED at the dead group members, and then Zalen's lifeless body.

She saw the one they called Hux sitting on the ground several yards from him, and also Elias, whom she remembered from those awful days gone by.

Elias tipped his hat to her.

Virginia looked at her hands, which were gripping her shotgun. At some point she'd recovered the weapon but didn't remember how or when. Both the shotgun and her hands were blurry and wavering like heat rising from a desert floor, and her body felt strangely adrift, as if floating and turning above the ground.

She saw Noah entering the woods to the west, moving with a purpose that confused her. What was he fixated on? Were more of them coming from the forest?

She opened the breach of her shotgun and withdrew the spent shell. It seemed too big to have been in the chamber, too wide or long or something. She patted her pockets, dragged her fingers through the dirt around her searching for fresh cartridges.

Then she looked back at Noah.

The forest.

. . .

THE FIRST MAN was easy enough to find. He was splayed out in the leaves, his pistol lying inches from his hand.

Noah picked up the revolver and spun the cylinder. One cartridge had been discharged, but the man hadn't been killed by return fire. He had a broken neck. That was easy to see.

The bullet he'd fired had entered a tree a few feet away and fresh blood was misted around the hole. There were no other bodies around, but here and there little scarlet droplets clung to branches, mixing with the leaves and soil leading farther into the woods.

Noah followed them.

He found the second man lying beside carved replicas of a house with tiny people standing in front of it—a shrine of some kind, or maybe a child's playthings.

Noah rolled the man over, thinking of the bullet hole and blood on the tree. But this man hadn't been shot either. Like the first, he also had a broken neck.

Noah looked around. The blood trail was trampled out here. A struggle, small broken branches and disturbed earth, several footprints. Someone had been on the ground.

The Cooper children had been here; that much he was sure of. But they weren't anymore.

VIRGINIA COOPER HAD DRAGGED herself onto the bottom step of the porch when Noah returned to the house. She was still gripping her shotgun and was struggling and failing to stand. When her eyes found him, she stared for a long time, the questions and dread obvious but left unspoken.

When Noah didn't respond, her body sagged and she began sobbing.

Noah knew those tears, knew the hell and torment they represented, and the bitter uselessness of them. He knew they were her soul dying and draining away.

And again, he reminded himself not to care.

A minute passed before her ranch hand rounded the corner of the house. The big man stopped and lowered his head. If the sight of her bruised and bloodied face concerned him, he didn't show it.

Virginia looked up at him. "The children?"

The man said nothing.

"Dammit, Cotton! Where were you? The kids were supposed to be with you."

"Yes'um."

"Don't 'yes'um' me! Where are my babies?"

Cotton didn't speak.

Noah noticed the blood dripping from the big man's fingers, and the bullet wound in his upper arm. But Cotton's head remained down, his body still.

Virginia pressed the barrels of her shotgun against the porch and tried again to push herself up. Again, it didn't work.

She looked at Noah. "I ... I just wanted ..." She held out her hands. "I just needed to—"

"Mama!"

Cotton moved away as the Cooper children emerged from the side of the house. After shaking loose from his sister's hand, the boy broke into a dead run, the girl struggling after him.

The girl was limping and the boy had been crying but otherwise both appeared okay.

As their mother pulled them into an embrace, the girl glanced up at Noah. There was relief and curiosity in her eyes, even thankfulness.

But all Noah McCreary saw was fear and confusion, questions and accusations, from another young girl somewhere far from home.

EPILOGUE

Virginia licked the paper and gently folded it around the tobacco, all of which quickly unraveled, fell apart, and scattered across the porch.

Cotton, who was sitting beside her with his carving knife and wood, moved to pick up the loose material.

Virginia waved him off. "Leave it be," she said. "Just ... leave it be."

The deep stabbing pain in her hip was worse than usual today, but still far better than the ordeal she'd gone through when Dr. Holland had wrestled the bullet out months ago.

Before beginning "the extraction," as he called it, Dr. Holland had warned her in his grating sing-song voice that, "Bullets coming out hurt worse than bullets going in."

And then he proceeded to prove it.

He'd also told her it was okay to scream, if she felt the need.

She had, several times.

When he was done and she was bandaged and laying in sweat, the doctor had gone on and on about the depth of mankind's depravity and the evils that compelled men to shoot up a woman and go after her family.

When Virginia only grunted, he asked how she'd single-handedly fended off a group of such men.

She politely begged off the discussion, referencing her pain and fatigue as an excuse for her silence. Which was convenient and also true.

Apparently, no one had mentioned a shooting outside the tavern the night before.

Apparently, no one had mentioned the name Audrey Mason.

VIRGINIA LEANED back in her chair, opened her tobacco pouch and took out another piece of rolling paper. She looked out at the corn crop which days before had finally begun to produce.

She'd been excited about the crop, as it was her first attempt at the vegetable—no small accomplishment for her. But just when the leaves were turning brown and beginning to dry out, she'd awakened to find the stalks trampled and crumpled, the ears sheared off at the ends.

She said, "That was a waste of good labor."

Cotton reached for the tobacco and paper.

She handed them to him.

Despite her injury, they'd made it through the late and difficult calving season, which was equal part miracle and equal part Cotton, if there was a difference.

Months before, she'd asked her father's longtime hand if he'd like to start taking his supper with the rest of the family. She'd set a place for him, even unpacked what remained of her mother's silverware—earning her a raised eyebrow from Piper.

Though it seemed trivial at best, it was the only way she knew to thank the big man, the only thing she could think to offer him.

The chair and table setting remained empty the first night and the first week. But Virginia continued to reserve a place for him, continued to extend the invitation during their breaks each afternoon.

The knock on the door came near the end of the second week, a rare but blessed rainy night they had both needed and prayed for.

She ushered him inside, not asking him to wipe his feet or remove his jacket, nor denying him seconds of the meal —earning her a raised eyebrow from Bran.

Cotton ate in silence, head down, big awkward frame in the small ill-fitting chair. Virginia noticed his hands trembling that first evening, which she knew wasn't from the rain and also knew she'd never understand.

But Cotton had returned every night since, recently even staying for a match with Bran at the checkerboard.

His quiet, reserved nature remained, but the shakes had diminished over time.

PIPER SLIPPED through the door behind them, brushed past Virginia without a word, and hurried down toward the well.

Virginia reached for her as she passed, but Piper was forty yards distant in a blink. Virginia hadn't even known she was in the house.

In less than a minute Piper was jogging back up the hill, carefully balancing a cup of water in her hands.

Her daughter had been wearing the same smile for weeks now, an absurd but infectious half-grin that never seemed to leave her.

Nor was it starting to today.

Unlike with adults, violence and tragedy didn't always cling to the young. Sometimes it did; sometimes it didn't. Or maybe it hid temporarily only to emerge later on. Virginia wasn't sure.

But then, perhaps it was something else entirely, she thought, as her daughter handed the water to Luke. Maybe it was that special magic in life that, for the young, was still so rich and mysterious, so mystical and new, that all else, even the most horrendous evils, seemed overcome by its warmth and light.

Virginia missed that part of life—the magic—missed it desperately. It was the best and most simple part of being alive. And she wondered why its endurance seemed so brief, why, over time, its allure and shine seemed to fade and wink out. She wondered if it had to be that way.

Luke received the water like a boy parched by the August sun, because he was. But as he drank, his eyes never left Piper's, and hers never left his.

The magic.

The boy was getting around now, though only for slow walks and brief periods. He was strong-minded like his father, and Virginia sometimes wondered if she was watching Ephraim at that same age.

She'd only learned of Luke's ordeal with Zalen a week after her own recovery began. And later still that Noah

McCreary had found him that night and delivered him to the doctor.

Doctor Holland had whispered to Virginia that the boy would probably never walk without the assistance of a cane. But Luke was gradually shedding his walking stick, especially when undertaking tasks he deemed important, like moonlit strolls by the river with Piper.

The teenagers turned as Sheriff Reeves let himself in through the gate and began the long walk to the house.

Everett had been by several times over the last couple of months, often accompanied by Theresa.

He'd said he received a telegraph from the new marshal, said a man named Noah McCreary was wanted back east on the charge of killing a deputy sheriff.

The sheriff had briefly looked around and then talked about the difficulties of being on the run these days, what with communications now being what they were. He'd also said he didn't figure anyone matching McCreary's description had been through these parts, which his wife adamantly agreed with.

And, in a sense, was true.

Noah McCreary was gone, had been since that day. Virginia never heard or saw him leave. She never got to thank him or ask why he'd come back.

The only reminder she had of the man who'd help deliver them was the dirty fist-sized rock with the golden-yellow veins she'd found lying on the table when Cotton carried her into the house that awful morning.

It was enough. It had to be.

Cotton said, "Them deers got 'em."

Virginia looked at him, but Cotton continued rolling the cigarettes. He'd finished three so far.

Virginia studied his big hands and fingers as they expertly went about the delicate task. Not for the first time, she found herself wondering what thoughts and musings existed inside a mind like his. She wondered if they might just be superior to her own, concluded they probably were.

She glanced back at the ruined corn crop, which he was referring to. "Yeah, I expect they did."

AUTHOR'S NOTE

I'm told people coming up from general anesthesia can sometimes be a source of great humor. My wife reports that after the first in a series of minor medical procedures I underwent, I woke, pointed matter-of-factly at her, and announced to the recovery room, "That's my wife!"

Embarrassing? I guess. But we were assured by the nurses that I was at least in good company.

The last of these procedures came a few years later. This time my wife says I woke, rolled my dreary eyes toward her, and said, "I'm looking for Mason."

Of course, I have no memory of any of this, but this Noah character had been whispering to me for some time.

At that point, I was disappointed and frankly burned out after writing a long and failed story over the course of several years. So I decided if I was going to do anything else (not an easy decision) it would be something shorter—a novella.

The idea of a small, isolated town overrun by a profes-sional gang had been with me for a while, but it was always missing that emotional piece I need to drag me through the difficult writing process.

So what about this Noah, I wondered? What if this was his story? The tale started to fill out as I thought about it, but even then it seemed too much to me like the typical western of yesteryear and was also still missing that certain spirit I was seeking.

Someone once described the storytelling process like building a campfire alone in the dark and then waiting to see if anyone shows up. I like this analogy—I also really wish I could remember who used it.

I decided to go with it, treating the story more as an experiment than anything else. So I made myself comfortable, tossed what kindling I had on the ground, and struck a match.

Virginia Cooper stepped into the light. I nodded and she nodded. Then she eased over beside me and sat down. And the flames began to grow.

I really hope this happens to me again someday.

As always, special thanks to my wife. This story would have remained nothing more than another musing of mine if not for her constant support and undying patience (she also discovered a glaring error that I had missed after multiple read-throughs, so if any plot or continuity problems still exist, please contact her).

And to editor C.B. Moore. A remarkable professional who not only brought her considerable knowledge and expertise to this little project but was a pleasure to work with as well—not always a common blend of virtues. Thanks for everything, Cee.

Any remaining structural flaws, poor grammar choices, and the like are entirely on me.

E.S. Taylor, 2022

Questions or comments? Contact the author at estaylorstories@gmail.com

ALSO BY E.S. TAYLOR

The Unknown

Printed in Great Britain
by Amazon